# FALLEN ANGEL

*A Dark High School Bully Romance*

## Jolie Damman

*"From the deepest desires often come the deadliest hate."*

— SOCRATES

# CONTENTS

# CHAPTER 1

## Change of Scenery

Okay, so I gotta look good for that party. A party, though? Huh, more like a business meeting inside my house. "It's a mansion, sweetheart," one of my maids told me one day, and I couldn't help but agree with her. I was rich, but I wasn't blind. I knew we were doing better in life than most people were.

One of the maids was combing my hair, and I was sitting on my very fancy chair in front of a mirror. I needed to look good for the party, even if I didn't care much for it. There would be powerful people in it, and me being the heir of the governor of California, I needed to look the part.

I sighed and said, "I can't even choose my own clothes and makeup."

"It's alright, though, isn't it? The fewer things you have to do, the better."

"It's not like that. I wish to be more active. All I do all day is to study and look beautiful for men who don't even care about me, at least not until I become a politician like most of them."

Celia was the name of the maid who was combing my hair and making it look perfect for the occasion. She chuckled before saying, "If you ever lose all of this, if you ever become someone more like me, you will miss this life."

I crossed my arms over my chest. "No fucking way. Not only there is zero chance something like that will ever happen, but I also will never miss all of this. I'm just fed up with all the bullshit, rich thing this and rich thing that. I need a breath of fresh air."

She stared at me through the mirror for a couple of seconds, surprised that I said those words. "Well, I'm just about done with your hair and then I will work on your makeup, so pretty soon you will have all the time you need to walk outside and breathe all the fresh air you need."

I uncrossed my arms and drooped my shoulders. "You are right. I'm sorry I sounded aggressive. It wasn't my intention. I just needed to say that being rich doesn't mean I can be happy."

"It's still a lot better than being poor. You have no idea how much money can help one person."

Some seconds of silence ensued once again. "We... pay you enough, right? If not, I can convince my mom to give you a salary raise."

She parted her lips, but didn't say anything for about five seconds, and then she spoke, "Y-yes, of course I'm paid more than enough. I love working here, and there is no company better than you, Ariel."

Ariel. Ariel Rummel. The last name of my family was known throughout the state, and most people knew who my mother was. Being the governor of California was no easy task to handle, but she was a master politician. People said she could even be the president of the United States, and I was sure she would, one day, try to be it.

She had the charisma and the money to compete against any candidate. The only questions were: would she want to govern over California for her second period or try for the presidency as soon as her current period as governor was over?

Celia finished combing my hair and then started to work on my makeup. We talked about random things, like how the school was filled with students who thought too highly of themselves. Some even bullied me, and I could never stop them. It wasn't really that bad. I kind of enjoyed all the attention...

But that was a silly thing to think about right now, and I was already thinking of reporting to the director of the school that those bullies needed to be expelled. I needed to do the right thing for once in my life.

Celia gave me a peck on my forehead and I then walked toward the main floor downstairs, where all the people were partying and making new deals. Hooray. I could almost not hold the urge to yawn right now.

I walked down the stairs, and most of the party attendees stopped what they were doing to stare at me. I liked being the center of attention, but these many eyes were far too many. I couldn't help but feel my cheeks warming up.

I walked through them as fast as possible without losing my grace, and found my mother. Her name was Desdemona. Not the nicest of names, but her charisma more than made up for it. A huge banner was hung way above her head, and it had a photo of her and her name. She needed to make people know where they were and who was the boss here.

Even though I lived with her my whole life, I couldn't help but feel out of place when I neared her and she turned her head to face me. We didn't speak about things concerning my life. The maids were the ones who cared about the difficulties I had and the battles I was fighting.

She opened a wide smile and leaned forward to kiss me on both of my cheeks. "You look lovely, Ariel. Haven't you already tried some of the delicacies that we are offering to my guests?"

"Not quite yet. I just came down here."

"Then, don't waste time," she said before turning her attention back to who I assumed to be a businessman. He was probably one of the most powerful people in the state, and mom most likely wanted to be on his good side. Lobbying was such a lovely thing.

I talked with some of the attendees, trying to keep my composure, and smiling all the time. I knew my smiles were coming off as fake, but who cared? We were all fake people trying to backstab one another. That's how it went with these parties for the rich.

I was bored to death when, all of a sudden, I heard heavy knocks on the main front door. I looked through the glass and my heart skipped a beat when I noticed the blinking red and blue lights.

The police? Here? What did they want?

A couple of guards rushed to the front door, and the whole party fell silent. It was so silent I could hear the beating of my heart, and that, in turn, made me feel more nervous than I already was when my eyes first noticed the blinking lights.

The guards talked to the police officer, who was a man that looked less than pleased to be here. Having finished talking with him, they rushed over to mom, and I was close enough to overhear them.

"Miss Rummel, he will talk to you only."

My mom's eyes widened, but she straightened up and said, "Okay, I will go talk to them and end whatever bullshit is happening here. I'm not allowing them to destroy this party."

She strode toward the main door as if she didn't have anything to worry about. If only she knew the bad feeling I had about what was happening, she would change her mind...

I didn't dare to walk over to them, but when the officer suddenly handcuffed mom, I had no choice but to walk as fast as my legs could take me. What was going on? I felt dizzy and the world around me turned into a blur.

When I reached them, my mom's eyes looked lost, and her face was pale.

"Mom, what happened? What is going on?"

"I don't know, dear, but they are taking me to prison right now. I trust you can take care of our home for me, please?"

Her concern was genuine, but our home soon turned out to be the least of our problems...

* * *

What really happened to cause such a turn of events, I didn't know, but the next morning, we had already lost everything. Celia was now taking me to my new home. A forgotten little house in one of the favelas in River Valley. I still couldn't believe what happened overnight.

Celia spoke, "Ariel, I know this is hard, but I will help you however I can. I can cook for you before and after you come back from your new school."

I heard what she said, but her words went through one ear and left through the other. She nudged me slightly to get my attention, and I finally turned my head to look at her.

"Like I was saying, I will help you however I can, but you need to promise me you will be strong."

"Celia, I don't even know what my life will be like from now on."

And I couldn't even move to live with a family member of mine. Mom didn't have good relations with them, and I didn't like them at all. Plus, living under their roof would only make things worse. They would think my mom then owned them something, and their price tended to be steep more often than not.

"It will be fine. I'm sure of it. I studied at that school you will go to, and it's a fine place. Not as... exciting as your previous school, but still a good place for a girl like you."

I crossed my arms over my chest. I knew Celia was only trying to make me feel better. She was a good woman, but right now, I needed someone who wanted to pamper me less.

"I'm going to live by myself and I will be forced to leave the house alone when I will be at school. Do you see how shitty that is?"

"I know, but you should control your language. It's not nice for someone like you to speak those words. You need to understand that Miss Rummel will be fine. I'm sure it's nothing but a misunderstatement."

I wished that was the case, but then she turned on the radio and a news presenter began to speak about my mom's case, "Evidence appears to be very substantial. She just can't buy off the legislative power which rules over the state of California. That is something we don't see in this country, and we can't allow it. We have to make an example of her case for any governor who might have the funny idea of doing the same thing she did. No matter how tough it might be to make the legislative power approve certain laws and projects, public money can't be used for buying votes."

He was right, but I didn't think that mom ever did something like that. I would have to talk to her, and tomorrow, I would meet her. It was a good thing that school wouldn't start until next week, and so I had more than enough time to get my bearings.

There was bright daylight when Celia approached the neighborhood where my new house was. So many houses covered the hill and, on the other side of the place, I could see the beach. It was almost like Rio, except that this was America.

How River Valley ended up having a favela was beyond me, and before now, I only saw it when flying above it in an airplane. The sight of it always gave me the shivers, and now it was like that feeling was multiplied ten times.

And I couldn't wait until the corruption case was cleared and I could head back home. I already missed the AC, the expensive food, the dinner table so carefully prepared by the maids and Celia combing my hair...

I guessed she was right. I would miss those things. I just never thought it would happen so soon.

Most of the houses couldn't even be considered houses in my point of view. Broken walls, walls that weren't painted and never would be, roofs that just straight up felt like they would crumble at any moment, and a high chance of catastrophic landslides...

But I guessed that the people here were in luck, in the end. It never rained enough in this part of the state for landslides to be a problem.

We crossed some streets, drove through the ocean of run-down houses, and I saw some shady groups on the broken sidewalks. People smoking and consuming drugs. Probably weed and cocaine and that sort of not very nice stuff for the body of a human being.

I sighed and the rest of the drive was a silent one, much to my happiness. I didn't feel like talking and I couldn't wait to lock all the doors and windows so that nobody would have the chance to break into my new home, after getting there.

I didn't think about this when choosing what to bring, but I brought the most expensive clothes and other things I had. A video-game console, my favorite makeup box, dresses and pants I loved to wear.

Some of the residents of this favela would be overjoyed to have those things for themselves, or steal them. At least tonight Celia said she would be with me, though there was only one bed and she said she wanted me to sleep on it.

I wasn't an asshole and I wanted to provide her with a bed, but there was nothing I could do about that. Plus, she said it wouldn't be much trouble for her. Celia also said she would take me tomorrow to see mom, so that was great.

It was almost as if nothing had changed, but then... I couldn't hold my tears anymore and began to cry. Noticing what was happening, Celia handed me a napkin, which I used to dry off the tears and control myself.

"Thanks," I said before handing the napkin back to her.

If it wasn't for her, I didn't know what my life would be like.

We reached the house, and it looked a little better than the ones that surrounded it. Of course, it was still so much worse than what I was accustomed to. Celia grabbed the luggage and headed to the door, and opened it, but I stood outside, just seeing what was around me.

This was not a place for someone like me at all, and I would be lucky if I came out of this place alive. I hoped nobody here knew me as well.

I stepped into the run-down house and could see all the rooms without having to walk much. There was the living room, the kitchen, one bedroom and one bathroom. The place was fully furnished, but the furniture itself was less than adequate.

I didn't want to keep on making comparisons with what my life was like before, but it was impossible to contain my thoughts. Everything changed so fast that part of me was still trapped in the mansion.

I barely had enough money for this place, but I guessed I should be glad I didn't have to sleep on the sidewalks like the homeless. *Things can always get worse.*

Celia showed me what she could of the place, and then made dinner for me. We didn't unpack most of the things we brought, and we would have to get the rest of the things out of their boxes later.

Dinner was fine, but I was tired and took a shower before going to sleep. I soon found out that the showerhead was broken and kept on dripping throughout the whole night, after I toweled myself.

I couldn't sleep at all, and in the coming morning, I didn't hear the chirping of the birds like I was used to. We had a huge garden with trees in our home. This place, though, instead of the singing of the birds, had people shouting all the time on the streets, as if those were their true homes.

I felt trapped inside my home, and during the night I heard people murmuring outside my window, and I was so scared I almost called the police. This favela was also the home of random gunshots and cars revving up and stopping all day long.

Definitely not the place for someone like me, and if these people knew who I was, I was good as dead.

Breakfast was dead, or rather, I felt like I was dead. I ate everything, but only because I liked Celia and didn't want to make her feel sad. Her cooking was still good, even if she didn't have all the fancy kitchen furniture and the best ingredients.

But anyway, that was far from one of the most important things in my mind at the moment. Celia took me to the prison and just being out of the favela was a nice thing, even if the prison itself was not a good sight. I didn't know how I would react to seeing mom in the orange clothes that they made criminals wear.

And she wasn't a criminal. It didn't matter what they found in the evidence, I wasn't believing them. Nobody knew her better than I did, even if we didn't talk much. I was still the closest family member she had.

Most of all, I wasn't going to abandon her, so whenever possible, I was going to come here to visit her, regardless of the consequences. What consequences? People at school saying things about me going to prison more often than a person like me should.

I didn't care about any possible consequences, and never would.

Celia waited in a room and I headed to another room where the prisoners talked to their family members or friends using a telephone. I sat in front of the glass which separated me from where mom would soon be sitting at, and waited.

Some minutes after, she showed up, but she didn't look her radiant, normal self. She looked changed, and not one full day had transpired since they arrested her. I wanted to scream, but something kept my mouth sealed.

She sat down on the plastic chair, and then picked up the red phone. I picked up mine, and she said, "Ariel, I'm so glad you came."

Her voice was weak, and I felt pity for her. "I'm sorry this has happened, mom. I want to do something to help you, but I don't know what can be done."

She sighed. "There is nothing you can do. Trust that my team of lawyers will be able to find out the truth and get me out of here. They confiscated most of my money, but I still have enough to pay the rent of the house you now live in and also their wages."

"But you shouldn't worry about me too much. I'm an adult now. I will finish last year of high school and I will find a job and we will have our normal lives back."

She chuckled, showing to me her light was still within her. "I'm so glad you haven't changed."

"And I won't. Not ever, and not because of some bullshit thing like the one they are accusing you of having done."

If there was a sign that, maybe, she was hiding something from me, I couldn't tell.

We talked about my new life, what it would be like to study at that school, my fears regarding my new home, when she could expect to be released, and how Celia would continue to help me out, even without the money to pay her the same salary she had before all of this happened.

Celia stood up once she saw me coming back and took me back to the favela. She didn't live in that 'neighborhood', but she lived closeby. The car was mine and she took a bus to head back to her home. Now, I was all alone, but thankfully, the school would start tomorrow, and perhaps... I would make new friends?

# CHAPTER 2

## First Day of School

The moment I stepped close enough to see the school and what it had inside its walls, I knew I was in trouble. Deep trouble. People looked at me as if I was a pile of shit on their sidewalk. They wanted to avoid me, but I wondered for how long that would be the case.

Usually, predators studied their prey before attacking. I hoped that was not what was happening here, but I couldn't know it for sure. Only time would tell.

At least I had my car with me, which I parked in front of the school. Not the best place to leave my only vehicle at, but I didn't have much of a choice. School wasn't too far from my new home, but it was still better to come here by car. That was something I couldn't lose.

I stepped into the school and hoped for the best. Students and even teachers kept on looking at me with wide eyes. I felt so out of place, and if only people here would look at me differently, I would feel a lot better.

Some students bumped into me, and I was sure they did it on purpose. Jerks. Just because I was new and everyone was already talking about me, they were already thinking I was someone they could stomp and walk over without consequences. They had a nice surprise waiting for them if they were thinking that was the case.

I eventually found my classroom and the teacher looked at me with wide eyes. Just like everyone else in this school, she didn't think someone like me would show up.

"You must be the new student," she hurried to get to me and grab my hand, and then took me further inside the classroom.

She made me turn to face the students, and I tried to hold my awkwardness. These moments always made me feel like that, and I couldn't wait to be done with high school so that I wouldn't have to endure them again.

*Why the hell do teachers still introduce new students in fucking high school anyway?*

"Ah, and I remember the board told me that you would come today. All your teachers have already been notified you would be studying with us. I'm so sorry about what happened to your mom," she whispered, but since the whole class was silent, there was no denying that every single student heard her words.

She turned to face them and straightened herself up. "Boys and girls, this is Ariel–"

"We know who she is," one of the students began to say, "you don't need to introduce her to us."

The teacher whose name I didn't know seemed kind of lost after that, and then she patted me on the back to tell me to find a desk. And that I did, and I tried to find the desk with the fewest students sitting around it. I didn't feel like mingling with them quite yet, especially now that the girl with red hair told me that everyone here knew who I was.

And considering that most students knew me now, it wouldn't be long before the whole favela would as well. Certainly not an ideal turn of events for me, but despite being pampered so much in my life, I grew a thick skin and could handle most of what this school could throw at me.

Classes were fine for the most part. I could hear my name being mentioned sometimes, but the students kept to themselves most of the time. I wondered when the bullying would begin. That sort of thing existed even back in my former school. It would be only logical to think that this place had even more bullies than back over there.

I headed to the dining hall. Calling it that was actually making it seem nicer than it was. The place was horrible, and even from the outside, the smell of the food that was being cooked was gut-wrenching.

But my growling stomach said I needed to eat and thus, after swallowing hard, I stepped into the 'dining hall.' Upon finding out that it was not buffet-style and that I would have been content with a single tray, I approached one of the cooks and asked, "Can I please choose what I want to eat?"

The cook, a big black man with a mean look in his eyes, narrowed his eyes and said, "No."

Someone behind me chuckled and said, "Don't mind her, Chuck. She is the governor's daughter and she thinks that this whole place should work for her. I don't pity her, and nobody here does."

I spun around and found none other than the same red-haired girl from my first class. She seemed obsessed with me, but for the time being, I wasn't going to waste a single second with her. Plus, my stomach was so hungry.

I refused to say anything and just got my tray and walked to the room where all the students and some teachers were eating in. I sat down, but when I tried to eat that food, I just couldn't. Not only was it worse than what Celia made for me in my new home, but it also didn't smell well too.

I ate what I could and headed out after leaving most of the food on the tray. Upon stepping outside, the same red-haired girl from class stopped behind me and said, "Hey, princess. Do you know that you shouldn't be wasting food?"

I controlled myself. I wanted to be pissed off, but I definitely knew I shouldn't draw the attention of everyone in here to myself, especially when most students were eating in the dining hall and could hear everything.

"No, it's nothing like that. The food just wasn't good today, I guess."

She approached me and I could smell her bad odor. When was the last time she used shampoo in her hair?

"Owwwn, and I'm just so fucking sad that our little princess is having some tough time getting adjusted to her new school. It must suck not having everyone treating you like a Goddess anymore, right?"

What could I even say to something like that?

But she continued, because she had to, "If you know what's good for you, you won't come back here tomorrow. This school is less than pleased with having the crook governor's daughter with us."

And with that, she turned and walked away. She wasn't alone. A bunch of other girls followed her, but then, one of them pushed me with force and made me fall on my ass.

I didn't cry, but I wanted to. I was trying to be tough, because this kind of environment forced me to be like that, and... I wondered for how long that facade of mine would last.

When I was trying to get back up, someone offered me his hand. Without thinking clearly, I took it and found none other than a very handsome boy about half a head taller than me. He had a pair of very deep blue eyes, and his face was buttery smooth. But there was something else in his eyes too, and it wasn't a pity for me.

Another guy was behind him and he was even taller, stronger, and he was also mockingly smiling at me.

I took a step back, and that was the spark the first one needed to speak, "*Princess Ariel*. What a surprise to finally make your acquaintance. My name is Blaze and this is my friend, Gabriel. He's Brazilian, so don't mind his accent, not that he speaks much, to begin with."

"Ahhhh... nice to meet you two, I guess," I said.

Blaze approached me so that his mouth was one inch from touching my ear, "I will reiterate Chloe's warning. Don't come back to this school, or there will be severe consequences. No one here will pity you."

And with that, he walked and bumped his shoulder into mine, making me stumble. Gabriel followed him, and they disappeared around a corner.

I certainly wasn't about to make many new friends here, was I?

* * *

Classes ended for the day and I wasn't about to do what those people wanted. I didn't have much of a choice, as else I would be back at my former school.

I opened and closed my locker after getting the books and some other stuff I needed when Chloe smacked the metallic surface beside me with her hand. I spun around in an instant to find her bright green eyes aimed at me as if she was about to kill me right here and now.

"Are you stupid?! We don't want you in this place anymore."

I didn't know what to say to make her leave me alone, but I did remember this, "You told me that you don't want to see me here tomorrow, and today isn't tomorrow."

"Owwwn, the little princess has grown a backbone, hasn't she? I wonder how long your tough attitude will last. No one who has been pampered her whole life can study with us a whole year and leave as the same person."

I felt that, if I talked back to her, I would only make things worse. And so I swung my backpack over my shoulder and started to walk away, but then two hands – probably from Chloe – pushed me with force and I tripped and fell over.

I didn't hit my head, but she managed to get under my skin. I was mad and frightened at the same time. Scared, yes. All this time I was trying to control my fear, trying to tame it, but it was here. It finally resurfaced.

I wasn't a tough girl, or at least, I wasn't beyond crying when my whole world turned upside down in less than a day.

And so, this time, I didn't get immediately back up, and let one tear escape the corner of my eyes.

Chloe squatted in front of me and said, "Seems that you are finally understanding where you stand at this school. Below everyone else, and even below the trash. There's nobody here to protect you, and we all hate your mother. Honestly, I hope she never gets out of jail."

At this point, I was trying to sit on the floor at least, but she pushed me again and then walked away. I tried to get back up and my eyes caught sight of Blaze as he came over to me with his friend right behind him.

He leaned on the lockers and crossed his arms in front of him. "Chloe really hates you."

I got up and said, "That's an understatement."

Now that she was not here anymore, I managed to be tough again, even if that was nothing more than a facade. I could be tough when the situation called for it, but not this tough and certainly not for such a long time. I was on the verge of breaking apart and crying.

However, since he was here now and also wanted to have his fun with me, I needed to be strong once more.

"Ariel, what do you even think you are doing in this school?"

"What sort of question is even that?"

"Someone who lost everything, but who is still a rich bitch deep within her heart shouldn't be here."

"It's not like I have much of a choice."

"Damn. Justice must really have done a number on you."

"What do you want? To mock me?"

"Something like that, and also to have my revenge."

His revenge?

"What did I ever do to you?"

"You didn't, but your mom fucked up our lives forever. Did you ever visit this neighborhood before it was turned into this?"

I didn't, but I remained silent anyway.

He gave me one slow blink. "Your silence is all the answer I need."

He approached me, but thankfully, he didn't murmur to my ear this time. But he still had something to tell me, "Humiliating you is so much better than seeing your mom in jail. I'm sure she will enjoy learning that her little girl is having a tough time at her new school."

And with that, he walked away, but without bumping his shoulder against mine. Gabriel followed him, still silent but smiling as always. Blaze was the scariest and the meanest of the two of them, but Gabriel wasn't too far behind.

They were definitely not the team I wanted to be near to, but they had a plan for me. What was it?

# CHAPTER 3

## It Gets Worse

I had dinner and this time, I was the one who made it. I did know a thing or two about cooking, but my skills regarding that weren't as good as Celia's were. It was no wonder, then, that I hated the pasta I made. And that was one of the easiest things to make for dinner. I definitely wouldn't try anything fancy until I could get a hang of how to use the stove as Celia does.

I took a shower and slept, and the coming afternoon, after classes were over and I had pretty much about the experience as on my first day, I walked over to the parking space where my car was and found it almost completely scratched.

What. The. Fuck.

Those students didn't do that, right? They couldn't have? But... *they did.* It was the only solid explanation. I contained my tears. I didn't want those people to think I was weak and that I loved that car so much.

It was the best thing I still had, other than Celia, after being forced to live in this favela.

I looked around, trying to find where those assholes were, because they had to be closeby. They would want to find what my reaction was like. I was sure of that.

Even though, on the inside, I was falling apart, I wasn't about to let them have more of what they wanted. Chloe and Blaze wanted me on my knees, crying and sobbing. Those things, however, they were never going to see me doing again. Not ever again.

I tipped my chin up and walked over to my car. I turned the engine on and drove away, not even bothering to look behind to see if they finally came out of their hiding places now that I wasn't near the school anymore.

Upon getting home, I collapsed onto my bed and wished for things to get better. However, if there was one thing that was taught to me, it was that they wouldn't until I did something about those bullies. What could be done, though? I didn't have friends at my new school and not even the teachers over there liked me. I imagined that was so because my mom didn't raise their salary when they asked for that last year.

*Whatever* was what I tried to tell myself, but I soon let one tear escape, and then another and another until I couldn't contain all the bad things that were being done to me anymore. I thought that this place would be the worst thing about living here, but the students were actually far worse.

The sun had already set when Celia showed up and found me like this on my bed. She hurried over to me and hugged me, and then said, "It's fine, Ariel. I'm sure you will eventually get used to your new life."

Having her with me again made me feel better, but I couldn't help but cry and sob again. She must have seen my scratched car in front of my house, so she knew how bad things were being to me.

But with her with me now, at least for tonight, I managed to recompose myself, and then she made me dinner and slept with me. She was like my second mom, and I was so glad I had her. Without Celia, I would have broken apart already.

The next school day was pretty much like the first two. Chloe didn't waste every single opportunity she had to mock me and spit her hatred for my mom at me. Blaze and his best friend also had their encounters with me, and even though I was feeling an attraction for him I didn't like, he was still the same asshole.

I could almost slap myself in the face for even feeling something like that for him. *Handsome, really, Ariel? You need to stop falling for the wrong kind of men.*

Ever since my former boyfriend, who was an asshole I loved, dumped me for two girls who wanted to 'share' him, I felt like I shouldn't try to love someone else. And that did work for a long time, until now, it seemed.

But whatever feeling I had for him, I could control. I wouldn't let my heart get the better of me again. What happened with my former boyfriend was a lesson well learned.

This time, when I walked over back to my car, I was stunned. I knew these people were jerks, assholes, and not good people at all, but I didn't think they were capable of doing *that*.

My car was turned over, the windows were broken and the tires were removed. Probably stolen. I hurried over to it, almost trying to find out if this was all a nightmare, and that maybe I was about to wake up from it.

But as the seconds passed, nothing changed and that was the confirmation I needed that this was real. I just lost my car. Who did it? I knew who, but I didn't have proof. I could call the police, but did they even come here to patrol this area, where the drug lords ruled over?

And now I would have to walk all the way back home. I didn't feel like taking the bus, and I didn't have cash for that. Even if I did have someone to borrow me a dollar bill, I didn't know if I would have the courage to share the same bus with those people.

My ears picked up laughter and chuckles behind me. Upon turning my head to find out who it was that was watching me, I found none other than Chloe and her group of bitch girls with her. Of damn course, and I was sure that, if I looked more carefully, I would probably find Blaze and Gabriel somewhere nearby too.

This was all their plan, and it was only getting worse. Should I find somewhere else to study and live? Not a chance that could happen. That house and this school had already consumed most of my money. I would have to endure this until mom's charges were cleared.

I breathed out and started to walk away from there. I didn't want another confrontation with that asshole, and I just wanted some peace now. Upon getting far enough from them, I rested my back on the wall of a house and breathed out. I just needed some seconds of peace.

And peace I got, but then, I heard the noise of a car approaching me. I opened my eyes and found none other than Blaze and Gabriel in it. I didn't even know they had a car. Their vehicle seriously needed to be repainted, though, and one of the front lights had long been missing.

They stopped the car and Blaze leaned toward me on the driver's seat, his forearm resting on the opened window. "Does our little princess need a ride back home?"

Jesus, even outside of the school they wanted to humiliate me.

I breathed out and started to walk away. I wouldn't say one thing to them. I was done talking to Blaze and Gabriel. Nothing of what could be said would make them hate me less.

But they wouldn't give up. They mocked me, sang and overall were assholes as they followed me back home. I guessed that at least they made the somewhat long journey seem less long than it was, since they kept my mind occupied with them.

When I turned the corner where my house was close to, they shouted, "Bye, princess!" and then drove fastly God-only-knew where, tires screeching. At least they wouldn't know where exactly I lived, but considering who they were, maybe they even already knew where my house was, what number it was...

I sighed, got home and found that Celia wasn't here. That was alright. I called the police and told them what happened to my car. They said they would take it and see what could be done, but considering that there were no cameras in the premises of the school, it was unlikely they would find the real culprits.

And I didn't have money for a new car, so hooray to walking to and from the school every day. That was going to suck.

❊ ❊ ❊

I was taking some of my books out of the locker when a heavy body collided against the metal, creating a ricochet of rattling noises. I gasped and tried to distance myself from that student, but then another guy grabbed the other guy's neck and a fight between them ensued.

Bone met skin, and kicks and punched missed and found their intended targets. Students from all over hurried to cheer and shout while the fight continued, and I was almost right in the middle of it.

I asked myself where the teachers were, since this school didn't have any guards, but it was Gabriel who pushed himself through the crowd and gripped the neck of one of the students. He lifted him up with ease and then tossed him against the lockers, the rattling noise filling the surrounding atmosphere once again.

The other student hurried to get out of there, and the whole place fell silent. Blaze, then, showed up out of nowhere, startling me and forcing me to take a couple of steps away from him.

The other students who were all watching the fight walked away and murmured among themselves as if what happened didn't matter much. It was a normal occurrence in this kind of school, it seemed.

Blaze approached me and said, "Gabriel here is the kind of guy that instills fear in everyone here, including the teachers. I told you that this place is not meant for someone like you. You are a princess. All you know is money and *more* money. I imagined you even have someone to wipe your ass, isn't that right?"

I didn't answer his question. How could I?

He shook his head, as if in disapproval. "Must have been fun walking all the way over here. How has it been trying to be more like one of us?"

His hand waved slowly and vertically once in front of me, obviously to help him make his question clearer. He wanted to find out why I cut holes and destroyed my clothes before coming here today.

I did that to try to blend in more with the other students, but since he asked that question, it seemed that it didn't help much. At least I didn't see Chloe today, so that was a relief.

And again, I didn't answer his question. I feared him. Blaze was no normal guy. He was the top dog in this school. He was even above the teachers.

He sighed. "I have a proposition for you. Something you might want to think about. Interested?"

Once again, I didn't answer. His eyes studied me for a second, and then he continued, "How about becoming one of mine, like Gabriel here? He does everything I want, and he is protected. People used to pick on him all the time when he first came, but because I now own him, they've given him peace. Considering that you are so poor you can't even find a better house to hide yourself in every night, you might want to consider my proposal. It would be better than being the center of attention of many students, including me, until your mom bullshits her way out of prison."

He lifted one eyebrow, waiting for an answer that I didn't want to give. He then shrugged and waved his hand to make Gabriel follow him. They disappeared around a corner, and I finally had some seconds to breathe and recompose myself.

I waited some seconds and then finally walked out of school, and headed back home. On the way there, I was glad that Blaze and Gabriel didn't follow me again with their car. I had time to think, and think I did.

To become one of his? What did that even entail? Would I have to become his bodyguard like Gabriel was? *Not a chance.* Blaze was tough and he didn't exactly need someone to protect him, so Gabriel wasn't actually his bodyguard. He was more like his pet.

And maybe Blaze wanted me to become his pet too. What would he even do to me in that case? Would he force me to have sex with him? Would I be allowed to drop out of our agreement if I so decided?

So many questions, but I couldn't deny that his proposal wasn't... too bad. I could be going crazy, but I was fed up with all the bullying. I was fed up with Chloe and her friends, and they had been bullying me every chance they got.

It wasn't a decision to make right now, and so I had dinner, took a shower, did my homework and plopped down on my bed. I was so tired and I wanted a moment of peace. I thought about his proposal, and I found myself increasingly more inclined to accept it. But first, I would have to know what it entailed.

I slept, but when the sky was nothing but darkness and stars, I heard the noise of glass being broken. My heart sped up, and I got off the bed and walked and hid behind the doorway. A man, huge and muscular, who wore a ski mask grabbed the TV and my console, and then got out through the broken window.

And just like that, someone just invaded my home and stole two of the things I loved the most. I was scared shitless. My mind thought about one thing only afterward, and so I made a decision. Tomorrow I would finally find some peace in my new, uninvited life in this hellhole.

*  *  *

I didn't have to look too hard to find Blaze. He and Gabriel stood beside their car, talking about something that seemed very important to them. Blaze was doing most of the talking, but Gabriel did speak sometimes, his th's either sounding exactly like d's, t's or f's, depending on the word.

Blaze turned his attention to me and tipped his chin up, and I said, "I accept... your proposal."

That was hard. I never thought I would bend the knee to someone like him, but I had to after someone robbed my place.

The corner of his lips curved upward as he smirked. "Good."

"Is that it?" I asked.

"Yeah, that is it. Just hang out with us. People will get the message."

"And what will you want from me?"

"That... you will find out in due time."

"So, you want me to be your pet and you don't even want to tell me what I will need to do for you?"

He approached me and said, "As I said, you will find out the answer to your questions in due time."

I was left speechless as he and Gabriel got inside their car. The sun was about to set on the horizon. Blaze turned his head to me. "Want a ride back home? No better way to tell everyone here that you are mine now."

Some seconds of awkward silence ensued. I didn't think that he would straight up offer me a ride. I was already dreading having to walk the 30 minutes that took to get home.

I couldn't help but think that his offer did make me think somewhat differently about him. He was still an asshole and he still instilled fear in me, but maybe, underneath all the pile of shit that covered him, he was a good man?

*No, Ariel. You don't get to fall in love with the wrong man again.*

"So, you coming or not?" Blaze asked.

Upon offering me the ride a second time, I got into his car and sat down on one of the backseats. Yeah, maybe this could work, and I was already feeling relieved that nobody would bully me anymore.

While he drove me home, he said, "So, what happened to your mom exactly?"

I was shocked that he brought that up, but decided to respond to him anyway, "You must have heard the whole story in the news, right?"

"I did, but that's only one side of the story. I want to hear the other side, your side."

I was even more shocked that he seemed so intelligent and intellectual all of sudden. The tone of his voice was different too. More friendly, more thoughtful, like he actually cared.

But he didn't really care, and I would do well to remember that.

"I don't know what happened exactly," I began to say, "but when we were having a party, the police showed up and arrested her. They think she bought off the state parliament to approve her projects, but I know my mom and I know she wouldn't do something like that."

"I see, but evidence seems to suggest otherwise, and many parliament members are saying that they did see it all happening. Obviously, those people did accept her money, which is public money, so it's not like they are innocent or anything like that."

Thanks to the rearview mirror, I noticed that he was smirking. He probably found it all funny, considering he wasn't the one involved in my mom's case. And fuck, I couldn't help but admire the fine lines of his face and his deep blue pair of eyes. He was so handsome. If only he wasn't such an asshole...

But I reminded myself I shouldn't let my feelings for him grow, and he dropped me off in front of my house after we talked a bit more about mom's scandal. He admitted to me before that he knew where I lived, so it was no surprise he didn't ask where my house was.

"Have a good night, Ariel," he said while waving his hand goodbye. Gabriel only looked at me with some interest in his eyes, but as usual, he didn't say anything. I didn't know if he was like that before he accepted Blaze's proposal, but his attitude was a frightening one still.

We talked about random things regarding the school and classes on our way here as well. It was almost like Blaze wasn't the bully that I knew he was. And I reminded myself, once again, not to begin to think he was anything beyond an asshole.

My deal with him had consequences, and I was sure that soon I would find out what they were...

# CHAPTER 4

## His Obsession

I guessed that I didn't think it would all be explained to me so soon. The moon was high in the sky when I heard a strange noise coming from outside my window. Celia was with me, but she was sleeping on a mattress she brought and placed in the living room.

With her in here, I was even more scared of something terrible happening. I didn't want to involve her with things she didn't have anything to do with. She was a nice woman and didn't deserve to have to babysit me because of mom and her stupid corruption case.

I sat up on the bed and had to cover my mouth quickly to muffle a scream when my eyes found him. Outside my window was none other than Blaze, and he was shirtless.

I knew that the temperature right now was a bit high outside, but I didn't think I would ever see him without a shirt on. And his eyes found mine, and through them, he spoke everything that I needed to know.

This was part of the consequences of being owned by him, wasn't it?

And to top it off, I wore nothing but my pair of panties. I hurried to cover my body with my blanket. The last thing I wanted was to let Blaze seem me naked. If he ever did, I would be so vulnerable to him I would never be able to stand up for myself.

His eyes studied me for a second, and something flashed in them. He was a smart man - probably even the smartest in the whole school - and I wouldn't be surprised if he knew I wasn't wearing much.

And without a warning, without asking for permission, he slid up the window and got inside my bedroom. Once again, I had to contain another scream. What in the world was he doing here?

Without saying one single thing to me, he walked around my bedroom, ignoring that I was awake. He checked and grabbed some of my things, and when he opened the drawer with my panties, even though I wanted to stop him as fast as possible and slap his face multiple times, I remained where I was.

But he didn't open the drawer, and then finally turned his attention back to me. He sat on the edge of the bed and said, "Nice to see you are awake, and wearing pretty much nothing."

I finally managed to calm myself down enough to tell him this, "What the fuck are you doing here?"

"Claiming what's mine."

Oh Jesus, he was confirming my worst suspicions.

"You don't own me."

"Well, if you want to end our deal right now, you can, but then all the students at school will go back to picking up on you every single day, and I'm sure you don't want that, right?"

I didn't answer him. I thought about Celia and that, if she weren't a heavy sleeper, she would eventually wake up and find out there was a shirtless guy inside my bedroom.

I couldn' help, though, but be aroused by what was happening. When was the last time a guy climbed into my room and was assertive with me? Never. It never happened to me before, and I was sure that Blaze knew that.

I hated myself for falling in love, more and more, with him. I shouldn't. The bad boys weren't worth it and Blaze was one of the worst of them I had seen my whole life.

He approached me more, and his lips were so close I could feel their smell. I could smell his breath of fresh mint. The odor of his cologne was intense in the air too. He took a shower and readied himself before coming here.

At least Blaze wanted to look his best.

"I need you to leave, Blaze. My friend will wake up and call the police if she finds you here."

"You have a friend? Do you mean that woman that takes care of you? She won't hear a thing."

Not true, considering how paper-thin the walls in this house were.

"Ariel, you have no idea how owning you makes me feel. There is something about that which makes me think you are nothing more than a trophy of mine. Imagine this. One of the former richest girls in the whole state is now my plaything. To top it off, I can have my continuous revenge against your mother. She will find out about this, you know, that you had sex with someone like me."

And just like that, he told me his plans. He never had any pity for me, not that I thought he had. He wanted me so that he could have his revenge and make him feel manlier or whatever it was that turned him on so much.

And the worst and most frightening thing about that? My clit was throbbing hard right now. I was fucked up in the mind.

"Why do you hate my mother so much?" My tone was not its usual, normal self.

He looked out the window. "You know this neighborhood. I bet you do. This place used to be something else, and then all sorts of people moved over here. It's no wonder that it became poor in a couple of years, and it was all thanks to your mom, who managed to raise the housing prices in other parts of the city. And there is also the fact she worked hard to end the only public hospital the state had. My mom needed that place, and when... she couldn't pay for the treatment anymore, didn't have a public hospital to go to, she died, and that's why... I want to see nothing but justice. I want to see your mom rotting in jail."

He didn't look at me, but I could see the gleam on his eyes. That was pure hatred. Not for me, but for my mom, but since he couldn't approach her, I was more than enough for him. A shiver ran down my spine.

"Well," he smiled and continued, "I shouldn't be saying those things to you. I came here for you, because now I own you, and I want you to give yourself fully to me. That's my final objective. When you scream my name as I bury myself deep into your womb and pump my cum into you... I want that to happen, and it will be so fucking good when it does."

I was afraid to the point of feeling my heart about to give up and stop altogether, but I also couldn't help but admit that he was making me hornier by the second. I always fell for the wrong kind of men. They just turned me on so much. I knew I should be looking for the nice guys, but they didn't make me feel like he was making me feel right now.

And when he turned his head back to me and I saw his eyes glinting with pleasure, I knew that he knew it too. He knew I had feelings for him, and that I was nothing but a trophy for him to conquer. Maybe he would be rough - and my clit was begging he would be - or maybe he would take his time. Whatever his approach would be, I was sure to become his little toy pretty soon.

"You can't force me to have sex with you."

He smirked. "I won't. Don't worry. I'm not a rapist. You know the only crime that not even criminals forgive? Rape. I'm a poor guy, but I don't do that sort of thing. I would never be able to sleep if I did, which is why I need to convince you to beg me to fuck you."

His smirk widened and I said, "If you think that has a chance of happening, you better consider your options. I'm never going to have sex with you."

"Here's the thing, princess. Your body can't lie, and that wet spot on your bedsheets tells me everything I need to know. I fucked many women and never paid for sex. I know I'm handsome and that women fall for me easily. All your former richness didn't prepare you for someone like me. You can hate me all you want for being overconfident, but let me tell you this as well: overconfidence is a virtue that few men can have."

And he was right. I tried to be confident far too many times in my life, only for then to fail again and again because I was too self-conscious of my looks and my decisions. I would never be as confident as he was, and that was... one of the many reasons that made me fall so easily for him.

Fuck, if I could slap myself multiple times in my face, I would have done so already. I needed to wake from this nightmare where my body was begging for him to take me. I hadn't had sex in years...

His hand grabbed mine, and he was gentle, and I couldn't help but allow my blanket to fall just enough to show him some cleavage. His eyes sparkled, and he continued, "See? I knew you weren't too hard to break. You can scream and call the police now, if you want."

But I wouldn't, and he knew that. What a bastard.

His hand was making me feel so fucking turned on. It was big and masculine, but at the same time, his grip was light and soft. His eyes were dark with his desire for me, and for a moment, I felt I didn't know this guy at all. Who was he, and why did he have such an obsession with me?

His hand caressed mine, and we continued to do that for what appeared to be an eternity. All the while, his eyes didn't stop staring at me. He was like a magnet, and I couldn't control myself. I was hating myself for having fallen in love with him.

That's what was happening here. I was in love with him. And I shouldn't, because he's an asshole who deserved the love of nobody.

His hand let go of mine and he started to massage my leg underneath the blanket. He wasn't being aggressive or anything of the sort. He was being caring to me, as if he wanted the best for me. But that was a lie. An illusion. He made his intentions clear to me when he explained his past to me.

And he then leaned forward, his lips approaching mine, and I thought we were going to kiss for sure, but then he pressed one of his fingers against my mouth, and said, "Not right now, and not like this. I know what I need to do."

He got off the bed and climbed his way out through my window, the unusual silence of the neighborhood making me super sensitive about myself and the environment that surrounded me.

What in the world just happened, and what exactly did I get myself into when I 'signed' that deal with him? Did it involve his friend also, or was he the only one allowed to take advantage of me? I shouldn't try to find that out. I should take advantage of the fact that was protecting me now, survive this one last year of high school, and then be accepted into a proper college where someone like him would have no place at.

I breathed in and out, trying to control myself, but I failed to do so. Celia was right in the next room, and she could have heard everything and decided not to check out what was happening. But most likely, she slept through his long stay in my bedroom, and since I was a coward, I wasn't going to tell her anything about what happened the following morning, and she would never know that the boss of my high school invaded my room and proved to me that my body wanted him.

And it wasn't just my body that wanted him, that it wanted him to bury his dick inside me, but also my mind. I was a fucked up gal. That I could never deny.

High school promised to be even more unforgiving with Blaze now thinking that he owned me...

* * *

The clock woke me up, and I took a shower and got dressed. Celia made breakfast for me, and I was so thankful she was here with me. I didn't want to spend hours thinking about what happened last night. Celia made me think about her, that she was here with me, that I was not alone, and because of those facts, I was so glad she never gave up on me.

And when I swung my backpack over my shoulder, ready to walk all the way to school, I heard a familiar honking outside my house. Celia raised an eyebrow, and I said, "It's only a friend of mine from school."

She seemed lost at my statement, but nevertheless resumed cleaning up the dishes and said, "I'm glad you've already made friends there. I thought you would have a hard time getting used to your new school."

She didn't know half of my story over there, and for her own good, it was better that way.

I walked to the door, opened it and saw his car. Blaze, as usual, was behind the wheel and Gabriel, this time, was sitting on one of the backseats. I approached them and Blaze said, "Come on in. We don't have much time. First class will start soon."

"Wait, you are taking me to school?"

He raised an eyebrow. "Of course. You are mine now. You do whatever I want, and I want to make sure everyone in school knows you belong to me."

Again, he had to remind me that I was his now. I needed to play cool with him, or else he could end our deal and I would become the subject of more bullying. What he was doing to me was still miles better than battling against a multitude of students.

I sat down beside him, and he drove toward the school. He and Gabriel didn't say anything, but their bodies did. They were relaxed. They knew this was their environment, and Blaze also knew that he now owned the daughter of the governor. That made him feel better, manlier even.

And his overconfidence turned me on too.

We got out of his car once he parked it, and we headed to class, once again without saying anything. Blaze was the one in the middle leading us, and all the other students looked at us with wide eyes. Some weren't as impressed, and those were the ones who already knew what changed between us.

Blaze walked slower than he needed, probably to make sure everyone got the message. The new girl, the daughter of the governor, was his now, and nobody could touch me.

I would be lying to myself if I said that I didn't enjoy the protection. It came with a high cost, but it was so much better to know that the other students wouldn't try to destroy me anymore. I was relieved, even though I knew that Blaze thought he owned me.

And did he own me? I was battling against myself to tell my mind otherwise, but on the outside, I needed to act as if I truly belonged to him now.

I just wondered what other ideas he had for me. He already invaded my privacy at night and touched me. I just hoped he wouldn't snap and force anything on me.

We stepped inside the classroom, and even the teachers were surprised I was with them. I sat near them, and I could hear some of the students murmuring my name. Chloe was less than pleased that she couldn't haze me again, and that was one of the things I liked the most about being 'his' now.

I had one of the calmest days at school, and the following days were very similar. Blaze would always come in his car to pick me up and drive me back home after the classes were over, and even though he didn't speak much, he was gentle and caring. I kind of liked the new him. He was an asshole still and I did well to remember that once more, but he was treating me as if I was someone he truly cared about.

He didn't really care about me, though. He was only trying to make me trust him, but that was something I would never do. I could never trust someone like him.

Over time, I cherished even more that all the bullying stopped. Most students looked at me with different eyes, like I was one of them now. I didn't want to be one of them, though, but there was no denying that gaining some respect in school helped me a lot.

Blaze didn't invade my privacy again like he did that night, and weeks had passed since then. I was kind of glad he kept me alone for the most part. During the breaks between classes, he didn't speak to me, but he always kept an eye out in case anyone wanted to torment me. However, since I was now their boss' 'protected one', nobody ever approached me to do something of the sort.

His protection came with another cost. I couldn't make friends, since people didn't want to talk to me much. I was alright with that, though. River Valley High was a temporary place for me until my mom's corruption case was resolved and we could have our things back. I was so sure she didn't do anything wrong. I knew her my whole life and I did go to her workplace often. She would never buy off anyone to make things happen the way she wanted.

However, just when I was getting used to my new routine, Blaze came to me intending to ruin that...

* * *

We were walking out of the school when he grabbed my hand and said, "We are going to chill out near the docks, and you are coming with us."

It wasn't a request, but a demand. I was his now, after all.

I nodded, but only because there was no point in trying to battle him. If he wanted me to come with him somewhere, then it was better to agree with him. His lips curved to form a smirk, and he gestured with his hand for Gabriel to sit on one of the backseats.

Sun was about to set in the distance, and Blaze drove us down there, toward the main docks. Why he wanted to chill out there of all places, I didn't know, but I would be lying to myself if I said I wasn't scared.

There was something about going to an unknown place that frightened me. At school, if he tried anything, if he forced anything on me, I could scream and hope that someone would save me. But out here, in these forgotten docks, there was nobody to stand in his way. Gabriel would probably help him, if anything.

If I thought the favela was the worst part of the city, then those docks were even worse. Destroyed walls, broken windows, structures that were forgotten by their previous residents, and a smell of dirt with something else created the perfect atmosphere for people to run their illegal operations here.

And maybe that was why he took me here. Maybe Blaze was finally about to tell me that he bought and sold drugs for a living. I wouldn't put it past him. His deep blue eyes scared me enough to think he wasn't only a bully, but also someone that should be locked up in jail.

He parked the car in front of a warehouse, and I was surprised the main door was still closed. But that was only an illusion, because Blaze soon opened it and stepped into the interior of the place, closely followed by his best friend.

He checked the place out for unwanted people, and that took no more than ten seconds. This warehouse had nothing more than a coffee table, an old couch and a chair. Blaze plopped down on the chair, and his hand gestured for me to sit next to him.

I froze, but not for very long. I reminded myself to do what he wished, and that he wouldn't force anything on me. He wouldn't have sex with me unless I allowed him to, and although I was less frightened of him now, I was still beyond thinking he would be anything more than an asshole to me.

Gabriel walked back outside and soon came back with a styrofoam box and a boom box. He put the first down on top of the coffee table, and when he opened it, I saw what it contained. Bottles and more bottles of beer. Not expensive brands, but probably good brands nonetheless.

And he connected his phone to the boombox, and then it started to play loud pop music.

I widened my eyes as I looked at the two of them. Blaze raised an eyebrow, and then said, "Don't worry. We two are over 21. You aren't, so all you will be drinking will be soda. Gabe, give her one."

Without saying anything, as usual, Gabriel grabbed a bottle of soda and tossed it over to me. I grabbed it as best as I could, and was relieved I didn't let it slip off my hands and fall to the floor. It was made of glass, and it would have broken into pieces easily otherwise.

Gabriel plopped down on the chair, and Blaze rested his arm around my shoulders. I was scared and this place was less than ideal, but I would be lying if I said I didn't like what was happening.

My body was still demanding for me to say those words to him. *Kiss me.* But I couldn't. I would be betraying myself if I ever did what he said I would do. I would never beg him to fuck me and to bury his cock deep inside my womb. That would never happen. It was a promise I made to myself, and also one I was willing to die for.

"So, Ariel, are you liking your new school?" Blazed asked while Gabriel continued to drink his beer.

I was going to ask them why they were still in school if they were over 21 already. I thought they looked older than their age, but I didn't think they could already drink legally.

"I guess. Kind of."

"It's not as expensive and fancy as your former school, so you don't like it much."

He sipped from his beer bottle while he talked to me.

"No, it's nothing like that. It's different."

"As I said, you don't like it because it's not as good as your former school. That's okay."

"That's okay?"

"Yeah, it is. You don't have to hide anything from me. Actually, if you do, I might get mad at you and you don't want to find out what I'm like when I get mad. Don't you agree with me, Gabe?"

Gabriel smirked and took a sip from his beer bottle.

"I didn't mean it like that. Everyone was giving me such a hard time when I became a student at the school. They don't even know why I am forced to study with them."

"Oh, come on, Ariel. You know those people enjoy having you around. It's like a toy they can't touch anymore. Before, they could do that, but not anymore. I own you now, and I like to remind you of that."

"Not that you have to," I rebuked.

He put down on the coffee table his now empty beer bottle, and then gestured with his hand for Gabriel to give him another, which he did. He opened it and said, "It's much better to be my girl than theirs."

I wanted to say that I agreed with him, but I couldn't. I didn't want Blaze to think he was actually being nice to me most of the time. This place was creepy and I could hear almost every single sound or noise coming from miles away before the boombox was turned on, but we were actually... chilling and enjoying each other's company.

This was what chilling was for them, and considering we would have tough midterms soon, it was no wonder they wanted to relax. And Blaze and Gabriel were relaxing. Their eyes were less alert regarding their surroundings.

"Ariel, I know you've fallen in love with me, and one day, you will have to tell me that out loud."

I looked at Gabriel, but there was nothing in him that could help me. Blaze said something important, and he wanted a proper answer from me, but considering the circumstances, what could I say that would satisfy him?

But since I had to say something, I hoped that my next words were good enough, "I don't know what you are talking about. You invaded my bedroom in the middle of the night while my caretaker was sleeping in the living room and then you did those things..."

"But I didn't force anything on you, right? I was careful. I sensed your arousal for me, and that was all I needed. A woman is truthful when she is vulnerable, and women are always more vulnerable at night, when they are sleeping..."

If Blaze intended to make me more frightened of him, they were working. I was already thinking of a way to make it so he wouldn't be able to open the window from the outside again.

And all of this was making me feel that we should clear some things up. "Blaze, what is the meaning of all this?"

He looked at Gabriel and raised an eyebrow, who shrugged. "The meaning of what? This meeting in these docks?"

"Yeah, you guys seriously come all the way here just to chill out?"

His eyes widened a bit. "Why not? This place is perfect for that. We don't have to worry about anyone interrupting us, and now I have a girl who I will break. That's what I want from life right now."

Why did I even bother asking him what this was all about. It was always about me. Maybe he wanted to make sure I would know how dangerous he was, in case I got too comfortable around him.

And maybe the most frightening thing was Gabriel. The silent follower that did everything his boss wanted. What was up with him? I knew he could speak, but his silence was disconcerting.

But Blaze was the one who got my attention right now, and I couldn't help but feel aroused by him. His presence was immense, especially with how his arms surrounded my shoulders and how he was acting as if he truly owned me.

If only he knew what was going on inside my head... but he never would. There was no way I would tell him that I thought I was still my own person, that he would never have any control over me, and that I only decided to be 'his' for now so that I could graduate from high school and leave that favela for good.

"You know, Ariel, you are one beautiful woman. I want you all for myself."

His hand caressed the back of my neck and also played with my hair. I was admiring him, and even though he was making me so wet my panties were probably soaked through, I didn't want to admit to him that I liked him.

I should never have fallen in love with him. I should be stronger and end my tendency to think that some men can be different and better.

"Blaze, stop that. I don't want to have to scream and run off."

"Oh, but you won't do those things, right? You wouldn't. I can see it in your eyes. You want me, and all you need to do is to let go of your old life. Give it up. It's over and your mom will spend some decades behind bars."

And after those words were said, I stood up from the couch so quickly he was shocked, spun to meet his wide eyes, and said so loud my voice reverberated throughout the whole warehouse, "That won't happen! Her charges will be cleared and everything will return back to normal."

He stood up and placed his half-full beer bottle on the table. "If you think that things will just go back to normal, think again. Nobody comes to live with people like me, in that favela, and leave as if nothing happened. Even if your mom bullshits her way out of prison, your memories will haunt you forever. I will be forever in your mind. I will be the only man you will ever want in your life."

I wanted to tell him that he was wrong, but his deep blue eyes removed any ounce of courage I had to do so. I couldn't pretend I could battle him and win. Not right now. My mind was still not molded for the kind of environment I now lived in.

I looked down, but not for very long. Blaze cupped my chin with one of his hands and forced me to look into his unforgiving eyes again. I could feel his hot breath and how he wanted to dominate me.

But he wouldn't... not until he thought it felt right for him. For now, I was still beyond his reach, but... for how long?

And I couldn't deny that I wanted to touch those lips of his. They were so full and looked so soft. I was killing myself on the inside for denying myself this growing desire in my mind to allow him more space.

That was like allowing a criminal inside my house, and despite how tempting it was to my fucked up mind, I was still lucid enough to keep telling him no.

"You will be mine one day. So mine you will be begging on my feet for a chance to suck off my dick."

His tone was soft, but incisive. I felt a rush of warmth in between my legs. He wanted me and he was working his way to make my mind allow my heart to speak. I couldn't control my emotions, but I could control my actions, my mind, and right now, I didn't want to give him another sign he was winning.

I was trying my best, but Blaze had the experience of a 35+-year-old man. His life in the favela and the fact that he dated so many women, old and young, molded him into the man he was now.

His hand moved away from my chin, and then he sat back down on the couch. He gestured for me to sit with him, which I did. I didn't have anything to say to him about what happened and for a long while, we didn't speak.

But the ice between us was eventually broken somewhat, and talked about mundane things, like school problems, and even Gabriel spoke sometimes.

Afterward, just when Blaze stood up from the couch and was ready to leave, his phone buzzed. He fished it from his pant's pocket and his eyes widened when he read the name on the screen. I couldn't read the name, but I was curious. Why did it shock him so much?

He turned his head to me and said, "Stay here and be silent."

His eyes found Gabriel, who was already on his feet and ready to follow his boss' orders. They didn't speak, but I knew that Gabriel knew what to do. His mission now was to make sure I would remain where I was, sitting on this couch that was probably almost as old as this city.

Blaze put his phone on his ear and when he walked out of the warehouse, I heard him saying 'hello', but then whatever else he spoke was too low for me to make out the words. He walked all the way to the end of the docks, where the ocean waves crashed continuously against the concrete.

Gabriel still sipped from his nth beer bottle, and he didn't have to worry too much about me. I wasn't crazy enough to think I could knock him out somehow and sneak my way to Blaze to find out who he was talking to, and what about.

But I was curious and I wanted to find out what made Blaze so serious all of a sudden. Come to think of it, maybe it was connected to his job. He never told me how he paid his bills, but he had to have his source of income, considering that I knew he lived by himself. One of the girls at school told me as much.

He talked over the phone for minutes until he finally came back. I was sitting on the couch still, trying to drink my soda and not trying to initiate a conversation with Gabriel, who himself was more worried about whatever it was that was going on in his mind.

Blaze came back and said to Gabriel. "Time to go. We have an important thing to do now."

He turned his head to me and said, "I will drop you off in front of your house."

I approached him and said, "Okay, but what is going on? Who were you talking to?"

"You don't want to know, and you won't know. Your job is to look beautiful to me. Don't think you are more than an object."

Despite being treated like trash again, his words caused a rush of warmth to harden my nipples. I wanted to slap my own face multiple times again.

And just like that, we got back inside his car and he drove me back home. The trip was shorter than before and he drove faster than he normally did. Whatever he talked about over the phone, it was important to make Blaze stop being Blaze. He was always composed and overconfident, but right now, even though he didn't change much, he changed enough to make me curious, not that I was brave enough to do more than to stand like an idiot in front of my home while he and Gabriel drove off God-knew-where.

Or was I courageous enough to find out what they were going to do?

# CHAPTER 5

## Don't Even Try

But I didn't try to find what he went off to do that night. I couldn't sleep, though. My mind kept on thinking about him, and even though I refused to do this, my hand begged me to masturbate myself while thinking about him. I was so fucked up in the mind.

There was a confusion of thoughts in my mind. On one hand, I hated him because he was probably the one who fucked up my car so much it was still being repaired, but on the other hand, he protected me and kept me safe from the other bullies at school.

And maybe he ordered Gabriel that night to rob my house. The guy who did it was huge, after all. However, I could never be sure who actually did that because the man wore a ski mask.

Maybe that was part of his plan to make me accept to be his. Blaze was not like all the normal men in the world. Once his mind was set on achieving something, he worked hard to do so.

And, to be honest, it was all working out for him. I did become 'his' now, and from now on, he only needed to give me reasons to think he wasn't the asshole I was so sure he was.

The next morning, he did show up in his ugly car and drove me to school. Like usual, we didn't speak, not that he needed to. Blaze was the kind of man that spoke without using his mouth more often than not. Those deep blue eyes still terrified me, after all.

But I also couldn't help but feel more and more comfortable around him, and this morning, when he honked in front of my house, I was kind of glad he showed up. I knew he would come. That was part of the deal, and it was nice to have a bad boy spending so much time with me again. And I just reminded myself not to let him know that I fell in love with him because that would be the end of me. It took me years to recover from my former boyfriend, after all.

I sat next to him and while he drove, he said, "It's very early and I think you didn't have breakfast yet, right?"

How he suspected that, I didn't know, but I nodded anyway.

"Good. Then, we are going to have something today I'm sure you will like."

I was curious to ask him where he was taking me, but I didn't open my mouth. Not only did he want to surprise me now, but I also had a feeling we were going to chill out again and he was going to show everyone that he 'owned' me one more time.

I still didn't think I really was his, but there was no denying that doing something different with him was thrilling.

And Blaze took me all the way to a Wendy's establishment. Back in my normal life, which now seemed like a thing from a distant past, I rarely had the opportunity to eat a Wendy's burger.

He parked the car in the parking space in front of the place and we got out of his car. We sat down at one of the tables and Gabriel headed to the attendant to make the orders. I asked him to order their most mundane burger. I didn't want anything fancy and too greasy before going to school. I did have some important classes I wanted to be ready for, after all.

While Gabriel waited for our orders to be ready, Blaze turned his attention to me and said, "So, how have you been enjoying the life where you have to do everything I want? You do realize I can just show up at your window any of these nights and claim you as if you were nothing more than an object for me to play with, right?"

Once again, he was putting me in a position that was tough for me to handle, and he was becoming a bit repetitive. I was the only one showing any sign of changes. At this point, shouldn't even a cold-hearted man like him be somewhat different?

His inquisitive eyes were cold and made me feel shivers down my spine. Despite thinking that it was better being 'his' than being the subject of bullying every single day, he was still an asshole. I wondered if he ever would become someone different.

Given those things, I decided to change the subject, "Thanks for paying for my bugger, Blaze."

My voice was almost monotone and sounded fake, but I still hoped he would follow the direction I wanted for this conversation. Every time we talked, it was like I was walking on a floor littered with eggshells.

"Why? It's only common for the guy to pay for stuff when meeting a girl. And right now, you aren't only mine, but also my trophy, and I want people here thinking I'm doing the best for you, despite how you don't deserve any of that."

I was curious. "I don't deserve to have a guy pay for my burger?"

His eyes shot wide. "Of course not! You are rich as fuck, even if that might not be the case right now and for the foreseeable future. Point is, people still think you are a rich pig and that you should be paying for your own stuff. I mean, just look at your house. It's better than most in the neighborhood, and you have a car, which is being fixed, I think, but that's fine. It doesn't change anything regarding what I'm telling you."

I remembered what my house was like, but I couldn't agree with him. In my opinion, it looked as bad as all the other houses in the neighborhood.

"You are making me feel uncomfortable, Blaze. How about having a nice conversation like two human beings for once?"

His eyes studied me for a second. "And you think we didn't have that all the other times I was with you?"

"Definitely not. You act like I am an object to you, and not a human being."

I began to notice the similarities between how he treated Gabriel and me, and they sent shivers down my spine. I didn't know if Gabriel was always like that, silent all the time and kind of weird, but if that was the case, then it meant that staying near Blaze for too long could make me more like his best friend.

Gabriel came back with a tray in his hands where the burgers and the fries were put on, but Blaze continued the conversation as if he wasn't even with us, "Gabe is a friend of mine and he's thankful he became my bodyguard. What I need is to make you mine so that you never think about going back to your normal life. By the end of the school year, you will want to be with me. I doubt you will want to return to that old mansion which was most likely bought with corrupted money."

I wanted to slap him so hard right now. Every conversation with him turned into some sort of accusation to my mom, who was not even here. It was almost like he was acting as the lawyer of the other party and I was my mom's only defender.

"If you think that my mom is really to blame for what happened, you better think again. When her case is cleared, I will be back to rub on your face the fact that you were wrong all along."

He burst out laughing, and some of the people near us looked at him with accusatory eyes. "Not a chance, princess. I'm sure they've got more than enough evidence to prevent your mom from finding a way out. Now, if you will excuse me, I'm hungry."

I breathed out in pure relief, and then proceeded to devour my burger and fries. For now, we could have some minutes of peace where I could collect my thoughts. Every time I thought he was being nice and we could be more than what we were, he found a way to remind me that he was a complete asshole.

Nevertheless, I couldn't deny that I still found him handsome and finding more about his life, every day, was bringing me closer and close to him, to his heart. Maybe one day I would figure him out and bring out his good side. Maybe, then, we could be more than what we were...

But until then, I needed to keep my guard up whenever he was nearby, and even when he wasn't with me.

We devoured our burgers and put the garbage in the bin. Blaze then said, "Time to head to school. It should be almost time for classes, but we will get there in time. Don't worry, princess."

And he kept calling me princess, as if I was less than him somehow. I didn't want to think about it this way, didn't want to add something else to the pile of things I had to worry about, but one day I would make him see me for the woman I was.

I wasn't as tough as he was, but I was no pushover, and the fact that I've managed to survive while being 'his' was proof enough of that. I would endure.

We had classes like any normal day and, as usual, Blaze took me home. For the next couple of days, nothing of importance happened, other than my less than pleasing conversations with him which allowed me to get closer to his heart while he threw accusations regarding my mom's case.

But then, something was about to change, and it wasn't for the better...

* * *

The sun was about to set in the distance when someone grabbed my hair and yanked me toward him or her. I screamed, such was the pain, and tried to free myself from the grasp of the stranger.

But when I found none other than Chloe, whose eyes were red with hatred for me, I knew I wasn't dealing with an idiot who, all of a sudden, decided to bully me even though I was protected by Blaze.

They were nowhere near me now. Actually, they said they would do something - whatever that was - before heading to their car. They told me to wait, and I was heading there before Chloe stopped me.

I still tried to free myself from her by using my hands and the weight of my body, but something happened with her that made her change. Maybe her mind snapped all of sudden. Whatever was the case, I needed to know the reason.

"Chloe, do you want to die?"

"What does that even matter now? You are his girlfriend, aren't you? He didn't make you his property, he made you his lover."

I knew what she was talking about and I was shocked that it bothered her. I never noticed any signs she liked him, but if there was a woman in this school that was just like him, it was her.

"You are getting it all wrong! He only hangs out with me and brings me here. We aren't dating."

She scoffed. "Like hell I'm going to believe that. You and him... I saw you two at Wendy's the other day, and he paid for your food."

I was shocked that she noticed he paid for my food and that I didn't notice her there. This school was full of bad surprises day in, day out.

"That doesn't mean anything. Do you even know what his plans for me are? He wants to break me, to turn me into his sex toy. That's what he wants to do to me."

But my words flew in through one ear of hers and out the other. She didn't care about what I had to say. Nevertheless, I wasn't about to be silent, since that would only make things worse. Silence was, more often than not, taken as a sign of acceptance.

"As if those things mattered. I know how to read people's eyes, and I know that you are in love with him. I can see it in your pupils and how they dilate when you see him. Your mouth might lie, but the rest of your body doesn't."

Once again, she managed to impress me in a bad way. I didn't know she paid that much attention to details. Whenever I was near her, I needed to be careful, and right now, while she was gripping my hair like this and making it hurt, I needed to be better than my usual self.

"Chloe, if you want him, tell him how you feel about him. I'm sure that's all you need to do."

"Liar! He won't have me. He only wants you now. You are the only one from this school he hasn't fucked yet."

And just like that, she made me even hornier for him. I knew that before she told me, but hearing it from her mouth like this made all the difference. It wasn't enough that he was a piece of shit, but he also fucked whoever he desired. I could be one of many for him, but there was something primitive about such a fact that made my arousal burn brighter. And I wished someone would punch me in the face right now so that I could stop thinking I needed to have sex with him, and that he could become my husband.

Those were things that just wouldn't happen.

I opened my mouth to try to convince her, but then I heard calm footsteps approaching us. When he spoke, I wasn't surprised, "Chloe, leave her be."

Chloe immediately stopped gripping my hair and I breathed out in relief. My hair and my scalp hurt. I was just glad he was here with me, even if that meant owing him again. Blaze's eyes were cold, and he came here to fix something he should have fixed a long time ago, it seemed.

He approached Chloe, whose eyes seemed vulnerable. Not only her eyes, but her whole body seemed incapable of being its normal self in front of him. I knew he was the boss of this school, but I didn't know he commanded so much respect in front of someone like Chloe. I thought she was her own woman, but it seemed that was never the case.

She grabbed his hand, but he withdrew it and sighed. "You know you are not supposed to mistreat her. She is mine now, and I don't like it when people don't respect my toys."

Again, he was reminding me of where I stood and who I was to him. Nevertheless, I thought I could feel something different about his voice. Maybe he cared more about me than he was letting on? A possibility, but I couldn't be sure about that at the moment.

"She doesn't deserve you, Blaze! She will turn on you the moment she has the opportunity for that. You need to dump her for good and allow the rest of the school to have their revenge on her."

"Not a chance. Not while I'm here. She is mine now, and there is nothing anyone in this school can do about that."

Chloe bit her lower lip, and I could see she wanted to say something else, but in front of Blaze, that was like punching a wall. Not only did he dominate her in terms of height and overall body size, making her look smaller than she was, but he could also control her mind. There was something sinister going on between the two of them. They had a backstory I didn't want to know.

"Fine," Chloe said before giving me a death stare and walking away from us as fast as her legs could take her. I was calmer now, but it would probably take me a while to forget the events that just transpired here. I still; couldn't believe that Chloe was in love with him and that she thought I was her competitor.

If only she would understand that Blaze didn't see me as his girlfriend. Like he said time and time again, I was his toy, even if he had more plans for me that were soon to make themselves known.

*　*　*

Blaze's car honked in front of my house, and as usual now, I was excited. It was Summer Break and I didn't have much to do at home. He did say we would do things together. A normal woman would be terrified to be with him, but considering my upbringing and how I was forced to live in this place in less than a day since the police arrested my mom, it was no wonder I felt different from some other girls.

And without my console and the TV at home, since they were stolen the first few weeks after moving over here, I didn't have much to do other than to eat and sleep while waiting for time to pass. Gosh, was my life depressive.

I walked outside and tried to open a smile, but Blaze was his usual self. Not smiling at all and drumming his fingers on the steering wheel. I sat beside him and Gabriel was, again, sitting on one of the backseats, his eyes looking out in the distance as if there was something important to see over there.

"So, what are we gonna do?" I asked.

"We'll go to the beach as I told you. You brought your things, right?"

I nodded. I brought a bikini and some other things, like sunscreen. Blaze wore a white t-shirt and shorts. He would only need to take off his shirt to relax at the beach while admiring the stunning view. This place had some amazing beaches and I wanted to visit them again. I didn't think it would take Blaze to invite me to have a proper reason to go over to one of them, though.

Blaze drove toward the beach, and on our way there, he talked about mundane things, but he avoided touching the subject of his life. I wanted to find out more about him, but so far, I didn't even know where he lived. I knew that it was further up the hill where the favela was, but I never saw his house in person.

Maybe one day he would be adventurous enough to show me his home. However, considering he said he thought my home was better than his, maybe he kind of felt ashamed of it and would rather not let me find out what it looked like.

I wished I could tell him that I didn't care about that sort of thing. Considering that he was the only person in that school who didn't want to kill me, I was kind of... becoming his colleague? Even if he saw me as a treasure of his, there was no denying that there was a certain chemistry between us.

He saved me from Chloe. Who knew for sure what she would have done if he hadn't shown up? Maybe she would have beaten me up. I was no pushover, but Chloe was tougher, stronger and taller than me. I wouldn't have stood much of a chance.

Which was why I was thankful that he saved me from her twice. She was the one most intent on destroying me the moment I first got to this school. She was the one who knew me and probably told everyone my real identity.

I was thankful to him and after spending so much time with him, and him taking me to school and back home every school day, I couldn't help but feel that there was a human being under the pile of shit that was part of his life.

And Blaze talking about mundane things, talking about his life at school, tests and his scores - that was all making me think that we could be so much more than what we already were. Maybe I was being a fool for believing a guy of his caliber would be more than a bully, but there was no harm in dreaming.

We reached the beach. It was one of the most stunning places in the city, and one I could never have enough of. The blue waters, the yellow-ish sand, and the people coming and going. Despite not being crowded, it gave off the vibe that it was a place that people sought to be at as many times as possible whenever they could.

We walked to the sand with everything in hand, and we readied our things so that we could spend some time here without having to worry about the sun. It was hot, so we more than needed the shadow cast by the umbrella. We also brought blankets to lay on and relax.

Blaze laid on his blanket under the umbrella, and Gabriel set off to do something I didn't care about. He was always silent and usually a non-factor during our meeting anyway. That was his normal self.

And I forgot to apply sunscreen on. Maybe I was so focused on Blaze I didn't remember to do that. But the blanket and the warmer temperature made me feel so comfortable I didn't think to get up and apply the lotion on me. Plus, under the umbrella, I could spend some minutes at least without having to worry about sunburns.

People walked by us, some asked questions, some wanted directions, and all I wanted to do was to forget all the stress that came with living in that favela and studying at that school. It wasn't just the bullies, Blaze, but also the teachers who were less than pleased to have me with them.

Maybe they were also in it to have their revenge on me, but regardless of that, I didn't want to show any weaknesses in front of them.

But when I thought I was going to fall asleep, despite being so close to Blaze, he spoke, "I want you to apply sunscreen on me. Don't waste your time."

Despite the aggressiveness of his demand, I felt something different in his voice again. Maybe I was wrong about this, and most likely, I was, but there was a chance that he was beginning to see me as a woman.

Spending time with him was making me see him under a different light, a changed tone, and so it was only logical he would also change his opinion regarding me.

It wasn't something for me to dwell on, so I stood up and grabbed the sunscreen bottle. "As you wish. I'm going to do what you demanded."

He smirked, and that kind of warmed my heart. It was the first time I felt comfortable enough to crack a joke with him, and he actually enjoyed it.

"Don't get too comfortable around me, princess. I might not bite right now, but I can do so, in the future."

"I think I will take my chances. I would rather be bitten than be depressive all the time, or scared of you."

"Never stop being scared of me. It's the only thing you've got to keep your guard up."

And he was advising me now on how to handle him. He didn't want to admit it just yet, but there was no denying that he was acting different toward me. I knew that he was only keeping me around mostly because he wanted people to know I was his, but maybe he was beginning to see me for the human being I was.

I got on one knee and began to apply the sunscreen lotion on his back. I couldn't help but notice and feel how hard his muscles were, how they seemed perfect, as if he was sculpted and not born like all other human beings were.

I knew I was treading on a complicated ground. I needed to remind myself that he was still the same asshole that kept on mentioning time and time again that I was nothing more than his toy.

But... how could I keep on reminding myself those things when he was such a gorgeous guy and I was so horny? I needed to control myself, and for the time being, it was working, but there was no denying that feeling my hand on his body, as I continued to spread the lotion, was making me have more wild thoughts for him.

And that was why he was right when he said I was wet for him that night when he invaded my home.

I was probably spreading more lotion than it was necessary, and by the time I noticed that, it was already too late and I made a little mess that I fixed as fast as I could. Maybe Blaze noticed it, maybe he perceived I spent extra minutes applying the cream because I didn't want to move my hand away from him, or maybe he didn't notice any of that and was actually sleeping now.

I couldn't be sure of that. He wore dark sunglasses and his breathing seemed normal to me. His head rested on a pillow, and despite the hardness of his muscles, they were not rigid. He was relaxed. Even if he were sleeping, Blaze knew there was nobody on this beach that could be dangerous to him.

I wished I could ask him to apply sunscreen on me, but considering I didn't want to wake him up, in case he was sleeping, I spread some of it on my hand and began to apply it on myself.

However, just when I was going to spread some of it on my shoulders, Blaze raised his head and said, "If you want it, I can do it for you."

I was shocked. He was awake this whole time, and so the chance was high that he noticed everything I was feeling when I was applying the cream on his body. I could never figure him out, and despite feeling I knew him better now, it was still only the visible tip of a huge iceberg to me.

"O-okay, sure. I would be glad if you did that."

"Lie on the blanket and allow me to do it, then," he said before rising to his feet and grabbing the sunscreen bottle from my hand.

I did as he asked, and he knelt beside me before he began to apply the lotion on my body. To say that I started to feel aroused would be a monumental understatement. It was one thing feeling his body with my hands, and another to have his hands massaging me.

I had to contain a huge urge to moan. What he was making me feel was like nothing I experienced before. I did come to this beach many times in the past, but never with anyone that could make me feel like this.

My clit was begging for him to play with it, and all I could do was to remain very still. Blaze knew that he had control over me, but I didn't want him to think I was so desperate for him. If he did find out, it was all over for me.

He would, then, win and would also have no more reason to keep on protecting me. He never said this out loud, but there was no denying that he was only defending me from other bullies because he saw me as a challenge. He wouldn't be satisfied with me unless I was on my knees, begging him to take me as no other man could.

Blaze finished applying the sunscreen lotion, and I felt his eyes watching me for seconds longer than he should. I knew he thought I was beautiful, but there was still nothing like having the full attention of a man like him on me.

It was no wonder a girl like Chloe fell in love with him. There was something about Blaze that few other men could have, and just like he said to me that night in my bedroom, it was his self-esteem. He could be overconfident, but that was so only because he was sure of who he was.

"Well, that's that, then," he said before putting down the lotion bottle and going back to lying down beside me. He rested his head on the pillow and seemed to forget about me, even though I kind of suspected he didn't.

Blaze was still thinking what it would be like to have me all for himself. He did own me, in a way, but he needed me begging for his love, for him to fuck me, and despite what my body wanted, I wasn't about to become a slut for him.

Some people left the beach and it seemed less crowded now. The sun was also not as hot as before and more forgiving. I thought it would be a great time to get into the water and cool down when Blaze rose to his feet as he grunted.

"Oh fuck, I think I slept too much."

I also got up. "No wonder. It has been some hours since we have been here."

"Really?" He checked his wrist-watch. "Oh shit, you are right."

I looked around and didn't see any signs of Gabriel. "What happened to Gabriel? I thought he would be back by now."

"He should have been back already, yes. I dunno what happened. He said there was an important thing for him to do. Must be related to our job. I don't care, really. He knows how to take care of himself."

I shrugged. I did find it odd that his friend just disappeared, but there was nothing I could do about that. "So, you want to cool down in the water?"

He wore his sunglasses, but the way his forehead frowned told me everything. He was surprised I invited him to do something with me. That was so unlike me, but today was never meant to be a day where I wanted to be his toy or object or whatever. I wanted him to think I was a woman worthy of his respect.

"Sure thing... But don't wait for me to save you in case you start to drown or a current takes you."

"Point taken," I said before smirking.

He smirked back, and we started to walk toward the ocean. The sound of waves crashing filled the atmosphere and they got louder as we approached it. No one here looked at me or Blaze. We were nobodies in this place, and that was such a refreshing thing. Everything here was so different from what I was used to at school, where being Blaze's protected one brought me more attention toward me than I was okay with.

We let the water of the ocean cool down our bodies. It was like being in heaven, and despite how strong the push and the pull of the waves were, I managed not to lose my balance, for the time being.

Blaze stayed near me, and for a moment, we didn't know what to do. Should we be holding hands or hugging one another? Not a chance. He might have gotten more friendly to me, but he was still an asshole.

An asshole I liked, but an asshole nonetheless.

We didn't have to do much in the water anyway, though. It was cooling and it made me feel like staying in it forever. It would have been better to have a proper boyfriend with me here, but there wasn't much I could do about that right now.

Blaze spoke all of a sudden, "Hey, wanna head deeper into the ocean?"

"Why?"

I was curious. Why did he want to head deeper into the water?

"Just feels like it would be better for us. So, interested?"

I thought about his proposal for a moment. Could it be too dangerous for me? The pull and the push of the water were already pretty strong where I was and I didn't want to put myself in danger when I didn't have to.

Nevertheless and despite how horrible it would be to feel like I owned him because something else, I decided to go. He turned and I followed him deeper into the water, hoping that I was right about this.

I felt the push and the pull of the water getting stronger, but didn't worry much. Worrying too much would probably make me make the worst decisions and end up needing his help. Definitely not something I wanted to happen.

And he finally stopped walking further into the ocean, and I was relieved. I didn't want to show him any signs I felt that way and kept on trying to play with the water. Maybe, by faking how I was feeling, he wouldn't find out I was scared shitless to be taken by a wild current that would sink me into the depths of the Pacific Ocean.

He smiled and I tried to smile back, but that ended up being the worst mistake I ever made that day. By trying to smile, I forgot to keep my feet planted into the wet sand and I then immediately felt the water pulling me away from him.

I gasped. Shivers ran down my spine as I thought that this was it. I was close to him, but I didn't think Blaze would have enough time to react. I felt my body kind of falling over backward as it was pulled more and more by the water.

Everything happened in slow motion for me, as if I was about to die for sure and not even my mom would know what happened to me. I stuck my hand out to try to grab his, because, at this point, he had already realized what was happening and the big mistake he forced me to make.

His sunglasses fell off his face and if he didn't manage to get a hold of me now, I wouldn't die while only thinking depressive thoughts. My life was a mess and everything, bar some exceptions, worked to make my routine a living hell, but I just discovered what I never thought I ever would.

His eyes were wide and permeated with shock. *Blaze cared about me.* That was almost enough to calm down my racing heart. I thought he didn't care about me, that he saw me as nothing more than an object, but that look in his eyes was more than enough to tell me that I was wrong.

Blaze was still the kind of man that put barriers to hide his feelings and true emotions, but for a brief moment, they were destroyed and he let out the fact that he didn't want to lose me.

Everything happened in slow motion for me. His fingers brushed against mine, and when most of my body had already sunk into the water, he actually... managed to grasp my hand and then he pulled me out of what was certain death to me.

He brought me closer to him, pulled me even more, and his shirtless torso touched mine. My breasts pressed against his skin, and I was still in shock so much I couldn't think straight. All I could do was to look at his eyes like someone who didn't know what to do with her life.

His other arm enveloped me as he held me so close to him I could feel the warmth that emanated from his body. There were real care and love in the way that he hugged me. He wanted to keep me safe and find a way to tell himself that he shouldn't feel bad about what just happened. I almost died because of him, after all.

And his arm finally moved back to where it was, and his grip on my hand untightened. The moment of absolute tension, confusion and chaos had already passed, and our minds could think about what happened, and what was happening now.

I moved somewhat away from him while keeping in mind that I needed to be careful where I was stepping into and where. His eyes changed and he looked like his normal self now. Blaze was back to being his asshole.

But that didn't matter much right now. He showed me in that instant that he was afraid of losing me, and that's not the kind of feeling a man has for an object. I was more than that to him.

Maybe he was thinking I could become his girlfriend, find the way to his heart, but that was most likely, at the moment, nothing more than wishful thinking. But he was thinking of me as a woman now, someone he needed to protect because there was no one quite like me in his life, and knowing those things made all the difference to me.

I wouldn't hate him as much from now on, unless he decided to give me very good reasons to change my mind...

"I'm sorry you lost your glasses," I said, trying to break the ice that formed between us.

"Nah, it's fine. I will just buy a new pair. I think we should leave the water and wait for Gabriel under the umbrella."

"That's a fantastic idea," I said and we started to walk back to the beach.

It was a fantastic thing to do right now because I didn't feel like spending one more second in this water. I almost died in one of the cruelest ways a human being's life can be ended, and the experience was something that would be ingrained in my mind for months. I would probably not be able to sleep tonight and the following day as well...

We reached the umbrella where we had also put a beach chair on the sand. Blaze sat down on it, leaned his back and closed his eyes as he began to wait for his friend to come back. There were two more chairs below the umbrella, but I decided to lay down on the blanket again and try to calm my mind down.

My heart was calm, but my mind was a mess. What just happened was enough to make my heart think that there was no reason to be afraid of Blaze, but my mind was a different beast regarding that.

Not only was I so close to dying, but Blaze also did the impossible and saved me. He almost launched himself forward to grasp my hand and then pull me toward him. He also hugged me to make sure I wouldn't slip and lose my balance again.

Those weren't the actions of a man who didn't care about me. I was just wondering now when he would finally let go of his ego and admit that I wasn't so bad after all. I was the daughter of a politician, of someone he hated, but I was still my own person, and I was different from my mom, even if I loved her.

The blue color that permeated the sky was soon replaced by the orange, red and gold colors of the sunset. I rose to my feet, wondering where Gabriel was and worried he might have gotten himself where he shouldn't. River Valley was no safe place for anyone, regardless of how tall and tough they looked.

But just when I turned my head to see if he was coming from the other side of the beach, I noticed him jogging toward us. I didn't know what he got himself into, but his clothes were dirty and his whole face was smeared with dust and dirt. Gabriel was up to no good, and despite knowing how dangerous that was, I wasn't worried. I was with Blaze and him long enough to have some guesses regarding their line of work.

"We have a problem and we need to deal with it right now," he said once he stopped in front of Blaze, who himself had already stood up and looked ready to leave the beach.

"Then, let's not waste any time. We'll drop her off in front of her home and we'll deal with the problem."

Blaze turned his head toward me. "It sucks that we won't be able to go to a nightclub near here, but I have something more important to deal with right now."

"It's fine, I guess. We did have a good time together, though," I said.

"Yeah, I guess we did," he said before we started to walk over to his car.

We got inside it and he dropped me off in front of my home, as usual. I watched as they drove off toward the other side of the city, where they were about to do God-knew-what. Once again, I was left wondering what their job was exactly. Maybe one day I would find that out, and maybe such a day was closer than I thought. Nevertheless, it wasn't something for me to worry about right now. My stomach growled and I didn't know what I would make for dinner.

Regardless of what their problem was, what happened today was more than enough to make me feel that there was something important growing between Blaze and me. I didn't want to let him win, but if I could find out he was a nice man under his bad-boy attitude, then I was willing to give him a chance.

That could happen sooner rather than later. It wasn't something I could predict. When I stepped inside my living room, though, all I could think about was what the next day held in store for me. Summer Break was far from over, and he did say he would come here again so that we could do something else together.

# CHAPTER 6

## What He Wouldn't Do

This time, Gabriel wasn't with us. What a relief. I knew that he was Blaze's bodyguard and also his 'best friend' - if one could even call him that - but it was refreshing to be with Blaze without someone else's presence.

Gabriel was a tough man to figure out, and to be honest, I didn't quite know if he was being genuine or not. Maybe he was lying about who he was? Who knew that for sure. I needed to keep my eyes well-open whenever he was around. I didn't want to be surprised in a bad way by him.

We were walking around downtown, taking in the cool air of the night and trying to find something to do here. "There are so many options and you don't know what you want to do?" I asked.

"It's precisely because there are so many options that I can't choose, and right now, I want to find something that will please me. I'm kind of tired of all the bars and nightclubs I've visited so many times already."

We had a lot of meetings since the beach incident, and I felt I was closer to him than ever before, though still not close enough to consider him a friend of mine, and even less so to think of him as my boyfriend. Nevertheless, our tone to one another was a more casual one now.

"Just choose anything. I'm so hungry right now. I didn't have dinner because you said you would take me out tonight..."

"Maybe you should have had dinner so that you wouldn't end up depending too much on me," he smirked.

"You know what? I'm going to find a place I like and you will have to go there with me so that you don't end up all alone in the middle of the sidewalk."

"Not a chance, princess." He gripped my wrist and pulled me to him before I had the chance to do what I had told him. "You are doing what I want you to do tonight."

"What happened to that thing about not forcing things on me?"

He gave me an incredulous look. "Not only were you stupid just now, but you also don't remember my words exactly. I didn't say anything about forcing any kind of thing on you. I was talking about sex specifically, and I'm still working on that."

"Doesn't seem to be working too well for you, does it?" I smirked, and a couple who passed by us looked at me with judging eyes.

"I don't have to hurry, princess. I have got all the time in the world, and my plan has been going well."

Oh shit, so he finally noticed that I was becoming more and more friendly toward him? I didn't buy him gifts, but I did antagonize him less when talking to him. The tone of my voice changed, I was less silent around him and more vibrant in the way I gestured when speaking with him.

But I didn't think he noticed those things to the point of concluding that him being nice to me was working in his favor. I knew I shouldn't let those things change how I look at him, but there was no denying that his stunning looks made such a thing impossible.

He had the looks and now he only needed to show me had the personality. I couldn't fall in love with someone that only wanted to hurt me, and so far, Blaze had shown me that, deep inside, he could be a different man.

But when I was going to say to him that nothing changed between us, a man, tall and muscular, slapped my ass and forced me to spin around to meet him. Blaze immediately got in between him and me, but the stranger wasn't at all worried about him.

The stranger had peaceful eyes and a smirk on his face that was difficult to ignore. He wore mostly dark clothes, and it was almost difficult to discern him from the surrounding darkness. We were at a point on the sidewalk where illumination was lacking.

"Get out of here, idiot, if you don't want to get beat up to a pulp," the stranger warned.

"Not a chance, asshole. You are not touching her again. She is mine."

"Oh, she is your girlfriend? Someone like you, who doesn't even have a proper beard yet, thinks that he can get laid? That's the best joke I've heard all day."

He burst out laughing, and I could see Blaze's shoulders tensing up. This wasn't about to end well for him. I knew that Blaze was no pushover, but the stranger had to be twice his weight. Plus, who knew how well he could fight?

I settled my hand on Blaze's shoulder. "I think... we better get out of here and find a safe place for us. I don't like this man at all."

He turned his head just enough so that the corner of his left eye could see me. "If you think I'm going to chicken out because of this guy, think again. I never chicken out."

Oh Jesus, of course he had to be all stubborn now, and of course I was worried about him. And I wasn't only worried about him losing a fight that was about to ensue, but also regarding what would happen to me afterward. I wouldn't have anyone to protect me from that stranger.

Of all the times that Gabriel had to be absent doing whatever... It almost seemed like Blaze didn't know much about Gabriel's activities when he was out on his own.

"Asshole, you better leave us be right now if you don't want me to wipe the floor with you," Blaze warned after turning his head up to face the stranger again.

I took a couple of steps back, and that was when the stranger landed an uppercut on Blaze that made some of his bones in his head crack. I heard the sound that made and my heart skipped a beat.

Blaze stumbled, and he tried to punch the stranger right back, but his fist only met the air. The stranger propelled himself forward and landed another solid punch onto his face, who now not only stumbled, but lost his balance and fell over.

"You are nothing, kid, and you will always be nothing," the stranger said before beginning to kick him again and again.

I began to cry and shout for someone to help me, which made the stranger turn his head to me. He strode toward me while Blaze tried to get back to his feet when the light of a vehicle illuminated where we were.

The stranger immediately hid his face by using his arm and ran away from where we were as fast as his legs could take him. Before I could even think in which direction he headed to, he was already gone.

My eyes delineated two figures that ran toward a particular alleyway, and their caps and uniform were unmistakable. They were policemen, and I was so glad they showed up. Blaze, though, was less than pleased they were here.

He had blood on his face and someone needed to do something to help him. I was the only one, but I was lost in what to do. I was no physician and I barely touched his body before. It wasn't like I was all intimate with him now. His broken nose and cuts on his face, though, told me I needed to take him somewhere where we had water, and so I found the nearest public restroom.

The light barely illuminated the place, but I could still see that the stranger did a number on him. His nose was broken. Blood oozed out of it. The region around his eyes looked swollen and purple-ish, and his hands kept on checking out the lower side of his torso.

That stranger could have killed him right then and there if the fight had gone on for longer. Blaze might not be thankful that the police showed up, but I was. I learned that I cared about him and that I valued his protection, even if he couldn't save me from everyone.

"Blaze, I'm worried. I need to find something for your wounds. You look like a mess."

"It's fine." He tried to stand up, but immediately sat back down on the floor. This restroom didn't have anything for him to sit on, and he didn't look capable of walking right now.

"You need to rest and wait until you can walk."

"It's fine," he gave me a death stare. Blaze wasn't about to become someone different from his normal self right now, even if that man beat him the way he did.

"No, you don't get to tell me everything is fine," I said, and his eyes widened. He didn't think I would show that I was worried about him. In this restroom, we didn't have anything that could be used to heal him. I didn't have bandages, and I didn't even have a piece of cloth to remove some of the blood on his face.

That stranger could have killed him if their fight had gone on for too long. I was so glad the police officers showed up and ran toward him without asking us questions. I thought that, for sure, they would send one of them to ask us what the hell happened back there.

But they didn't, and now I was all alone with a man that made me feel so conflicted about him.

"You don't need to care for me right now. I will call Gabriel and he will help me."

He fished his phone out of his pocket, but I grabbed it from him and said, "No, you don't get to make all the decisions right now. You need someone to help you now, and that someone is me."

Blaze chuckled. "After everything I've done to you, you are acting as I treated you like a real princess."

"Say what you want, but I know I'm not an object to you anymore."

"Think whatever you want, princess, but you are mine and that won't change anytime soon."

Even when he was all beaten up and couldn't even stand up, he was still being an asshole. However, I needed to do something about all his blood. The bruises we could heal with medicine and ice once we were back home.

With that in mind, I took off my shirt and started to use it by rubbing the regions where there was blood on his face. I didn't consider the consequences of that particular action of mine, but his eyes did widen again. He didn't think I would be so comfortable around him as to show him my almost fully naked torso.

Cleaning the blood off his face made me feel better about myself, and it was worth it, regardless of what that made him think about me. I didn't care if he kept on saying that I was nothing more than a trophy to him. That was far from the truth.

"This is about as good as it gets, and now I will call Gabriel to come to pick you up. I could carry you to your car, but you are too heavy. You will have to wait for your bodyguard to come."

"Bodyguard and best friend," he corrected me, showing me that he did care about Gabriel. I never saw him showing any signs that he thought much about his supposed friend. Their friendship was kind of weird regardless, though.

Gabriel's number was easy to find. It was the first on the most used list, and he picked up his phone seconds after I started the call.

"Hello, Blaze?"

"Gabriel, it's me, Ariel. Blaze and I need your help. We need you to come to the public restroom by the entrance of Mission Beach. It's the one we used back on that day we went to the beach a couple of weeks ago. I think you remember it, right?"

"Ahhhhh, sure do. What happened? Why do you need my help?"

"Blaze... he decided to be all tough and acted like an idiot in front of a stranger who wanted to force me to have sex with him. It turned out that the stranger was quite the fighter and Blaze didn't stand much of a chance."

"Fuck, really? I will be right there with you. Don't worry, it won't take me long."

"Thanks, we will be waiting."

I turned off the phone and handed it back to Blaze. "Did you really need to tell him so many details about what happened?" He asked.

"Uhhhh, I don't see why not?"

"He doesn't need to know someone beat me up because I was protecting you."

"As if he wouldn't already know that you care about me."

Blaze chuckled. "You are in over your head if you think you are anything more than a trophy to me. I will claim you as I did to so many other women. All the ones in school fell on their knees and sucked me off."

"Even when you are in no position to be all tough, you still think you can do anything."

"That's how I am, and I won't change anytime soon."

* * *

The door opened and Gabriel stepped in. His eyes widened and he was shocked to have found Blaze incapable of walking by himself. Nobody came into the restroom during the time between after I ended the call I made to Gabriel and him coming here, which was great. I didn't want people to find out I was taking care of him in this restroom.

Gabriel's eyes flickered over to my shirt, which had now smears of Blaze's blood. He didn't make any questions and immediately helped Blaze get back on his feet. Blaze's face winced often in pain, and I felt a bit sorry for him.

He got all beaten up because of me and that spoke volumes about him.

Gabriel helped to take him to his car, and he sat on the passenger seat by the steering wheel. Gabriel began to drive and he took Blaze to his house, and that was the first time I was seeing it in person.

It was a run-down house like all the others in the favela, but there was something different about it. Something about that particular place resonated with the kind of man that Blaze was. Overconfident, an asshole more often than not, but still a man which deserved to be respected.

Gabriel took him inside, and I helped him by opening the door and keeping it open. Blaze's eyes glanced over to me, and he said, "Princess, you don't need to help me this much. I can do whatever I want."

"Even though you didn't drink anything, you are acting like a drunken fool now," I said, and he rolled his eyes.

We had become more friendly to one another, but maybe I was stepping where I shouldn't. Blaze's mind was a complicated one. Even when he was thinking I could be more than what he kept on saying I was, he didn't want to admit that he liked me now.

I could be making far too many assumptions regarding his life, and maybe that was a bad thing, but Blaze did make me think about him more than I should. He kind of was a puzzle for me to solve.

Gabriel grabbed what he could from the kitchen, the bathroom and Blaze's bedroom, and then helped to heal his wounds. Blaze didn't have much in his place which could help him with his bruises, cuts and the rest of the blood which I wasn't able to clean off him, but he did have bandages and some medicine for the pain.

"Let me heal myself, Gabe," Blaze said while sitting straight on the couch and grabbing the box which had the bandages.

He applied them where he had been cut, and that included his chin where the uppercut made contact. And then, he took medicine for the pain and looked at us with wide eyes.

"What are you two still doing here? I have better things to do now than being with you."

I chuckled and walked over to the door, and I was closely followed by Gabriel. "You take care of yourself, and don't be all grumpy all the time from now on just because you needed our help."

"Like hell I needed your help with anything, princess. You just wait and you will see the sort of thing I have in store for you."

And I hoped that wasn't a warning for something horrible. Maybe I crossed a line or two because I treated him too much like an equal to me, but I didn't want him trying to humiliate me again.

Gabriel closed the door behind him. "I will drive you home and then come back here. Blaze might think he doesn't need anyone right now, but I know that he needs me."

I put my hand on his chest and made him stop. "What's the deal between you and him? What did he do to make you so loyal to him?"

He raised one eyebrow. "What do you mean? He is a friend of mine, and we have known each other for a long time."

Ah, so it made sense now, somewhat, at least. "I see. I was just curious."

We walked over to the car, he turned on the engine and drove me home. He dropped me off and before he could drive back to Blaze's house, I said, "Thanks for driving me home. And take care of Blaze for me, please."

Gabriel chuckled. "You like him, don't you?"

I took a step back. "No, of course I don't."

He smirked. "You can't lie to yourself. I might not talk much, but I observe."

And with that, he left me speechless on the sidewalk. He knew a lot more than he was letting on, and I was beginning to think if maybe I should press him for answers. Answers to what questions? Like how he and Blaze met, and why he really was so thankful to have him as his friend.

They had a history, and maybe I would make him talk about it.

# CHAPTER 7

## Sparks and Fire

Summer Break was over, but my body still sweated a lot after walking outside for prolonged periods. Checking out the temperature always made me feel depressed, so I stopped doing that. Despite living in California, the sunny state, I much preferred colder regions and the snow.

I knew we had the mountains and that I could visit them to experience the snow and the coldness, but nothing beat living in a region that snowed a couple of times each year. I heard so many funny stories from people whose regions were affected by excessive snow and how they had to plow it and clear the roads so that people could live their normal lives.

I didn't have an AC unity in my house, and despite having Celia with me, it was a mess. My clothes were everywhere, and a lot of them needed to be washed. The problem with the latter was that, since I didn't have money to buy a washing machine and there was no laundry place near here, I needed to wash every single piece of clothing I had by hand, and that wasn't nice.

I wasn't lazy. I knew I had to, but I just didn't feel like washing my stuff right now.

And I was so fucking tired too. I could barely keep my eyes open. The thought that Blaze and Gabriel didn't have anything planned for tonight also didn't help things. I could be going crazy for good this time, but I wished he would just honk in front of my house and demand for me to go with him somewhere. It sure would beat spending another night in here reading a textbook. That was all I had to pass the time before midnight, which was when I usually went to bed.

The thought of having classes in the morning, in those old and forgotten classrooms, with people that still didn't like me, and dealing with teachers that didn't care about me at all made me wish there was a virus that would force the school to cancel all classes for the rest of the semester.

But that wasn't going to happen, and so I was left with just me and this house I didn't want to spend another second in.

I took off my clothes and turned on the showerhead, letting the water warm up before I could step under it. Once it was warm enough, I let it soak my body and my hair before applying shampoo on my hair and beginning to clean my body with a block of bath soap and a sponge.

I didn't turn on any music to help pass the time, and I focused mostly on the acting of taking a shower until I lost the perception of my surrounding environment. Despite how terrible this place was, at least the bathroom had a shower booth that was separated from the rest of it.

And I thought I heard a sound coming from inside the house, but I didn't think much of it. It could have been a cat running on the roofs of the houses as it tried to find food for the night. Stray cats were abundant in this favela, after all.

But then I heard another noise, and now I needed to stop my shower and pay attention to what was happening outside the bathroom. Maybe someone broke into my home to steal whatever else I had?

I didn't have many things one could steal, so his or her adventure inside my home would be a short one at best, and he or she would leave without many things.

I didn't hear anything else, and so I turned the showerhead back on. The warm water made me forget the strange noise in a matter of seconds, and I hummed while I rubbed my scalp to better spread the shampoo.

Minutes might have passed since the strange noise happened. At this point, I didn't care about how much water I could be wasting. The shower was one of the few things that provided escapism for me.

But then, all of a sudden, the door of the shower booth slid open and I gasped when I found none other than Blaze standing in front of me! Not a lot of time had passed since I helped him when he was beaten up by that stranger when we were chilling out downtown, and I didn't think he would come tonight...

He looked better now, and he had a devilish smirk on his face. If this was his way of sealing the deal with me, turning me into his forever, and making me beg for him to fuck me... it *could* work, depending on the execution of his new little adventure inside my house.

"Blaze... what the hell?"

He leaned his arm on the shower booth. "Just seeing what I've been waiting for all this time."

"If you think I'm giving myself fully for you today, you are completely wrong."

He chuckled. "Ariel, I think it's time you stopped lying to me."

I turned off the showerhead and was happy I managed to clean off the soap before he showed up.

"Considering who is saying that, I think you should be the one who shouldn't be lying anymore."

His eyes narrowed and he lost some of the coolness that was so characteristic of him. "I haven't told you one lie this whole time."

"Yes, you have. You keep on saying I'm nothing more than an object to you, but I'm more now, am I not? I'm someone you want to have as a woman and not as a trophy."

His eyes grew more alert, but he still responded like his normal self, "I don't think you understand why I've come here."

"Oh, but I think I do. You wanted to impress me and see if I was going to go on my knees to suck you off. I think I've got better plans for tonight."

And I was impressed I was using that tone to talk to him. The days where I was the submissive one to him all the time were gone already.

"That's only part of it. I've come here to claim you for myself one way or another, and since you have grown more accustomed to me, I don't think you will be able to resist. You will beg for me to fuck you and you will scream my name multiple times."

I couldn't deny we had grown closer to one another since we met for the first time. That night we chilled out inside that warehouse at the forgotten docks, when he took me to the beach, and when he saved me from that stranger were only examples of how much progress we had made.

His eyes danced around my body, looking and admiring each of my curves. I knew he was attracted to me, but I didn't think he would just show up while I was still taking a shower and not even bother to knock.

Like he kept on telling himself, I was his, and my house was also his, and so, from his point of view, it wasn't an invasion of my privacy.

Nevertheless, what he just did and kept on doing did make me hate him more. But, that was a fuel for something else. My whole body and part of my mind begged me to make the decision they wanted me to make.

They wanted me to become his. However, I wasn't about to let them win that battle. I did think that Blaze was a better man under the pile of everything that defined his bully side, but to be his, I wanted to continue being an independent woman too.

I wanted to be on the same ground he stood on. Being his submissive trophy was out of the question.

"And you think that sneaking up on me like this was a good idea? You don't even realize how much I hate that."

"I do, but I also know something else about you, and I can prove it by doing one simple thing you don't even suspect..."

"And what would that be?"

This whole time, I was naked and didn't even bother hiding my boobs and pussy from him. What was even the point. Blaze was the kind of man that got what he wanted, when he wanted.

And so, I wasn't surprised when he straight up cupped my cheeks and landed a solid kiss that I, indeed, didn't suspect. I thought about how wild it was and how it came out of nowhere, and he did... surprise me in a good way.

I tried to walk out of the shower booth with him, but Blaze used his weight and pushed me back inside it. I should be angry that he was kissing me without asking for my permission, but that was unnecessary, right? I knew why he kissed me all of a sudden. He knew I wanted him, and thus making love with him wasn't forced at all. It wasn't against my intentions. Deep inside, I had always wanted him to fuck me like this, and the best part about all of this? It was that he was treating me like a real woman.

His touches and how he kept me pinned against the glass wall of the booth were indicative enough of that. If I were nothing more than his trophy, something for him to use and discard without a second thought, then he would have straight up made me go on my knees and demand me to suck him off.

Blaze's kisses were dominating and endearing at the same time. There was a connection, a love bond that was strengthening and growing, and it would soon be so intense that we wouldn't be able to contain it.

His hands slid up and down the sides of my torso, and he kept me so occupied with his immediate kisses I didn't know what to do. I could be on the same ground he stood on right now, but he was still the one on top, and he enjoyed making that fact known to me. Blaze was the kind of man that needed to establish his superiority to other people whenever he damn pleased.

I reminded myself that I should be angry that he was such an asshole still, but that was a lost cause in my life. No matter how much I tried, I kept on falling in love for the wrong guys and although Blaze wasn't the first, he was the man that made the fire within my heart burn like never before.

His shirt got wet where he touched my breasts as he pressed his torso against me, and despite being aware of that, he didn't care. His body continued to grind against mine in a pattern that was so difficult to control and follow. And he didn't stop his kisses, which were now treating my neck with his raging fire for me.

I tilted my head and felt my whole body giving up. I was tense the whole day, but in a matter of seconds Blaze made me feel like one of those monks that don't have anything to worry about. Despite his intensity and how his body was all over mine, I felt calm and serene.

I moaned his name, and drove him to grind his body against mine with greater intensity, and I almost felt like I couldn't breathe anymore. But breathe I did every time he moved his head away when he was tired of kissing a particular region of my body. My mouth, neck and breasts felt so sore and loved at the same time after all those kissing sessions he made use of to assault them.

And I felt his hotness, his breath as he kissed and devoured me, and I also felt as his hands made it impossible for me to move my body. He was all over me like a lion that hadn't eaten for months. His hunger was like nothing I had experienced before.

The bad boys that had sex with me in my former school? They didn't hold a candle to this man. He wasn't just one of them, but also so much more it was difficult to describe who he was.

And when I thought I was going to die because he was making me feel an overload of sensations that were difficult to control, his body finally relaxed, stopped moving, and he moved his head away from me.

"See? I get what I want, and you, my princess, is mine from now on."

I breathed in and out, trying to control myself, and then said, "And I get what I want to. Since the first day we met..."

"Since that day?" His tone showed a genuine surprise. He never suspected I fell in love with him back then. It was a long time ago, but I imagined that, just like with me, he didn't forget what our first meeting was like, even if he thought I was nothing more than a girl who didn't deserve his attention.

I nodded my head. "And all this time, it didn't bother you the fact that you fell in love with the daughter of the governor you hate..."

"I still hate her and still think she is a crook, but you... you are someone different. You are your own woman."

"And just like that, you admitted that I'm not your object anymore."

He smirked. "We'll see about that."

In an instant, his kisses resumed and he was grinding his body against mine once again. All the air I had in my lungs was taken from me, and I thought I was going to die once more. His fervor and arousal were even greater this time, and his hands were all over me in a way that made it difficult for me to do anything other than to melt before him.

And here I was thinking I would be on his level, standing on the same ground as him in terms of how tough we were. Those things were never going to happen, right? I was his woman now, and although I still tried to take control of things, I cherished being treated like this.

There was no bad boy in this world that could do the things he was doing to me.

And when I thought we were going to do everything here, he picked me up with ease after we spent more minutes kissing and feeling one another. I gasped, but his kisses soon resumed while he took me to my bedroom.

He gently put me down on my bed, and then was on top of me in an instant, his body grinding against mine once again. My eyes caught sight of the wet spots on his shirt and pants where he touched me. He was the one who dried the front of my body, and now, laying on the bed, I was drying my backside. I wouldn't even need a towel once we were done.

There was no point, though, thinking about frivolous things when this young man was so dominating and he had all the energy in the world to burn with me. His desire was more than evident, and when I noticed the familiar glint of plastic sticking out of the pocket of his shirt, I knew that he came prepared for this and that we could go all the way.

I couldn't be the only one not doing anything here, and so I looked for the buttons of his shirt. Upon finding the first, I undid it, and then worked on the others, telling him that I wanted to feel his raw body against mine.

Blaze was no idiot, and he soon noticed what I was doing, despite being so occupied with my breasts and my pussy, which he was already playing with his fingers. He removed his shirt and tossed it over to the other side of the room.

His kisses soon resumed, but they were more varied this time. He even nibbled my ear lobe and murmured suggestive things this time. Just when I thought I was getting accustomed to how he made sex with me, he made sure to show me that I knew next to nothing about him.

And that was the truth, wasn't it? He knew so much about my life and I barely knew what his house was from the inside.

But that sort of thought was far from being one of my worries right now, so I pushed it away and hid it where it wouldn't disturb me.

I felt the hard lines that defined his muscles. Blaze was no muscle junky, but he was fit. His muscles were well-defined, and he was hairless on his chest. There was a happy trail that led to his cock, and it caught my attention as if it was the only thing that mattered now.

I worked my way toward his cock, but his hands gripped my wrists, stopping me. I questioned with my eyes why he was doing that, but he only shook his head, and then proceeded to kiss me as if he hadn't just destroyed the expectation I had built this whole time to find out what his manhood was like.

But considering how hungry he was for me right now, maybe he only wanted to take his time. Maybe Blaze only desired to extend this moment with me for as long as he could because, perhaps, he wouldn't have another chance to fuck me like this soon.

Everything was happening so fast that I was thinking things that didn't have a chance of happening. Blaze would be with me now all the time, and since I lived alone, he and I could have all the time in the world to have more hot nights like this one.

His hand then caressed and played with my pussy, leaving no room and space for my clit to breathe. It couldn't be controlled, and the more he rubbed it, the more I felt my orgasm coming. It was building up to become one of the most intense climaxes I ever had in my life.

I moaned, loud and louder, murmuring his name and grunting every time he nibbled one my hard nipples. Blaze was everywhere most of the time, and sometimes, he was just one man who found a woman that could be the right one for him.

I was aware he fucked many women before me, and none of them became more than sex toys for him, but I had a certainty in my mind that I was different to him, that Blaze would come looking for me again because he wanted to be with me.

Maybe it was only wishful thinking, but there was no problem with dreaming too much, right?

I didn't have time to think too much. Blaze stuck two of his fingers inside my pussy and made it his by rubbing it and using his fingers inside me the way that pleased him the most. And he was the kind of guy that liked to multitask. While he teased and tormented my cunt, he kissed my breasts and bit my hardened nipples.

My body shook, and I knew my orgasm had finally exploded. Even while he kept his two fingers inside my womb, I cummed. His fingers and his hand were coated with my juices, which he didn't forget about. He brought his hand over to his mouth, and he sucked the substance clean. Blaze didn't waste one single drop.

And that turned me on so fucking much.

His attention was on my nipples again for a moment and after having climaxed for the first time this night, I was more self-conscious about what was happening. My hand reached for the zipper of his pants like a thunderbolt this time, and I opened it before he even had time to notice what I was doing.

When he sat up, I gripped the waistband of his pants and tugged it down to his knees, revealing his pair of briefs and the man tools that he hid underneath it. His eyes showed his surprise, but not in a bad way.

He liked that I was finally becoming more audacious. If I could tell this to him now, I would have said that I became braver because of him. Blaze showed me that it paid off to be bad and bold sometimes.

He removed his pants and also his pair of briefs so fast the clock on the bedside table didn't even make its common ticking sound. Sensing where this was going, I gripped his member with force and established my dominance over him.

He showed me his big member as he thought he was going to end me right now, but little he did know that I also had my own plans for this moment.

I took his monster cock inside my mouth, and began to bob up and down along its length. He was so massive, and he was so thick. His pre-cum oozed as if his penis was a broken faucet. The taste was slightly reminiscent of what I tasted when I gave my former boyfriend his first blowjob.

Thinking about my previous hot sex nights, I wondered if I should tell him a little secret of mine, or if it was better to let him find out the truth on his own. There wasn't much to think about, and so I decided a matter of seconds.

I sucked him off until I left his monster cock redder than when I saw it for the first time. His chest heaved after the experience he just had. His eyes went wide, and they were indicative of one very important thing. He never had someone give him a blowjob the way I did for him.

Maybe he never had someone who actually loved him. At least, not like I did.

His eyes studied me for a second until he finally grabbed his condom package, ripped it open and slid the plastic along his raging erection. I watched as he did that, his movements happening in slow motion to me.

And when he readied himself and his eyes found mine once again that night, while crickets chirped outside and the favela was silent for the first time in weeks, I opened up myself as much as possible for him.

This was going to be rough. I had heard far too many tales to know what I was about to feel.

Blaze pressed his erection into my pussy, and he met some resistance. I was wet and ready, but of course, he didn't think I was a virgin. His eyes widened even more, and I had to say, "Just push it more... Don't worry..."

Poor Blaze was probably confused about a lot of things. His mind was most likely thinking about how I could be so experienced with sex while still being a virgin. I did have my experience with my former boyfriend, but we never made love like we were doing now.

His thrusts were powerful once he picked up his pace, and they continued to make me move and also make the bed creak under our combined weight. What before were confused and shocked eyes were now all the proof I needed that he knew what he wanted out of me, and that I would cherish what our relationship was going to be like from now on.

Blaze finished off inside me, and we snuggled up together. His lips lingered on mine as we fell asleep. What was going on in my mind right now? So many things it was difficult to isolate one. I thought about what our life would be from now on, and had hoped that he would be the man of my dreams, even if I also was thinking I shouldn't fall for the wrong man again...

What I didn't know, though, was that my world was about to be shaken up and changed forever...

* * *

The light of the sun met my eyes when I opened them. I was still in the same bedroom, the same house, but the environment that surrounded me felt so much better. What a night of sex couldn't do to a woman, huh.

I found Blaze, whose bad-boy face made me feel like kissing him again. However, I refrained from doing that. I didn't want to wake him up, and his closed eyes looked tired. It was probably a long time since he had a good night's sleep.

I couldn't believe I just let him take me the way he did. How could I have thought he would invade my house and steal my privacy when I was taking a shower? It was for those reasons, though, that I fell in love with him even more.

And I couldn't deny that I still hated myself for letting him find his way to my heart. I should be dating someone nicer, not the bully that thought of me as an object. As if I could control what my heart wanted to feel, though. Wasn't that the case with every single woman out there? I was sure it was.

Well, whatever was happening between us was too good for me to ignore or change it. I sat up on the edge of the bed and felt so lazy. I didn't want to get up and make breakfast. Now that Blaze was sleeping on my bed, I would have to make him breakfast too, which, even though it was a nice thing, made me feel even lazier.

I breathed in hard and stood up. When I was almost at the doorway, I heard something buzzing. It couldn't be his phone, right? I looked around the house, in my bedroom, and found where the sound was coming from.

His pants were shaking, and it had to be the phone the one doing that. Someone was calling him, and considering he didn't have many friends other than Gabriel, I concluded that it had to be him.

I was so lazy I decided not to pick up his phone and tell Gabriel that Blaze was with me and sleeping in my bed. I also didn't think that would be the right thing to do. Didn't know what his bodyguard and best friend would think of him staying the night at my house. He did suspect that I was in love with him and, given that, maybe it was better to keep him in the dark, for now.

I went over to the kitchen and made breakfast. I didn't know what he liked for that, and so I made the most common kind of breakfast for us. I did have a tray which I could use to bring him his breakfast, and so I used it to take the food to my bedroom, but I stopped when the phone buzzed again.

I put the tray on top of my bed and decided to pick up the phone this time. I needed to tell Gabriel to calm down and leave Blaze alone for the next hours or so.

My eyes landed on the name the screen of the phone was showing, and I almost let it fall off my hands. That name... it couldn't be. It didn't make any sense. It was him... the lieutenant governor of the state. What. The. Fuck.

Lieutenant Governor Joseph Wadkins was calling Blaze, a student that didn't have anything to do with politics, wasn't important anywhere else other than in this favela and the school he attended, and who also shouldn't matter one bit to someone like the person who now ruled over the state of California.

A wishful thought crossed my mind, and it lingered there. It didn't want to move away. Could it be? Could that be the whole reason why mom was involved in her corruption case? Could all of this be connected in a twisted way I could never have imagined possible before?

But just when I was going to decide what to do with the phone and the call, Blaze grunted as his eyes fluttered open. Quickly, I put the phone back inside his pocket and did my best to hide the fact I was nervous. I didn't want to make him think I knew what I now knew.

He sat up on the bed slowly, back resting on the wall behind him, and smirked. His voice was lazy, but he spoke anyway, "Didn't think I would find you awake right now. I wanted to snuggle with you a little bit more."

His nose sniffed the smell, and his eyes found the tray with the burrito and orange juice on top of it. His eyes widened. "I didn't think you would make breakfast for me. I'm so fucking hungry right now, though, so fuck it. Give it to me."

I didn't even have time to tell him anything regarding the call. He grabbed the tray and devoured the breakfast in a matter of minutes. I watched him as he did that, and for a moment, I almost forgot about the call and Lieutenant Governor Joseph Wadkins.

Blaze wiped his mouth clean with the back of his hand, and then gave me the tray. "Thanks for the food, princess. Should have come here before for dinner or lunch or whatever. Your cooking isn't too bad."

If only he knew what I knew, I was sure he wouldn't be so casual to me right now. He still acted as if we didn't just have sex and had become so much more than what we were before. Maybe that's who he was and even if he considered me his lover now, he would still treat me like his princess, a possibility that I was... actually fine with.

There was something about being treated as less than who I was that turned me on as nothing else did. But I quickly reminded myself about that number, that call, and put aside my relationship with Blaze for the time being.

I couldn't tell him what I knew, since I didn't want him to get mad that I grabbed his phone and discovered something about him I shouldn't.

But the call and what I found did change how I saw Blaze. I thought we had only a happy future ahead of us, even if it included many bumps along the way, but the name on his phone's screen changed that by quite a lot.

I still felt that he was the right man for me, but I had my worries. I needed to find what his connection with the new governor was. Ever since my mom was locked behind bars, he became the ruler of the state. It was a position I was sure he cherished.

If he had anything to do with my mom's corruption case, then I needed to find out the whole truth.

Blaze wouldn't want me snooping around his private life, even if I now was part of it. His job was something he kept a secret from me. Never once did he take me with him when he needed to 'work', never once did he even tell me one thing regarding that, and never once did he suggest he would tell me what his job was.

I was in the dark and finding out the truth behind his job, whatever it was, was going to be tough, but as I remembered the name on his phone's screen, I knew I didn't have a better choice but to go behind his back.

Would he be mad if he found out I wanted to know what was going on in his life when he wasn't with me? Definitely. Absolutely. His eyes would probably get red with hatred for me if he found out what I knew and what I was thinking of doing, but risking what we had built so far between us was way better than pretending that I couldn't help my mom.

Blaze enjoyed my breakfast, and I sat beside him on the bed. I kissed him again, and he got off the bed and put his clothes back on. When he grabbed his phone and saw the two calls he missed, his eyes lost the joy they had.

He was his serious self now. "I'm sorry, princess, but I've got something important to do now. I will see you later."

We kissed and he got back inside his car, which he parked in front of my house. I watched him as he drove toward where his house was located, and I wondered how I could find out more about his private life when he wasn't with me.

There had to be something subtle and sneaky I could do. If I could have a serious and long conversation with the current governor, then maybe I could make him spill the beans. Or maybe not. If he did what I thought he did, then he wouldn't be stupid to reveal his plans to someone who wasn't even half his age.

My approach needed to be smarter. If Blaze and Gabriel were meeting with the governor every once in a while, then there had to be an opportunity for me to tail them and find out what their meetings were about.

Acting governor Wadkins still had many enemies, I imagined, and it wouldn't be far-fetched to think he was preparing the ground for the next elections. Removing competitors? A possibility. It could also be that he was trying to find ways to kill and remove witnesses that would speak in favor of my mom.

I needed to be calm and rational from now on, and I was thinking I already knew a plan that would work. As long as Blaze didn't find anything about it...

* * *

The more I thought about it, the more it didn't make much sense. Did Blaze hate my mom to the point of offering his services to the acting governor so that he could have his revenge? Was evidence planted, or was mom in the wrong all along? I didn't think the latter was the case, but things were changing so fast. It would be more prudent to review some of my previous conclusions.

Maybe Blaze was always in the business of invading other people's homes to steal their stuff or to do whatever his clients wanted, and perhaps Joseph Wadkins found out that about him and decided to hire him.

Considering how much he hated my mom, maybe it was a no-brainer for him to accept that job. He couldn't have known I would end up becoming his classmate and his lover, but to be honest, those things didn't matter right now.

I never tried to make him stop hating my mom. The topic was brought up many times, but his mind seemed dead-set on thinking that she was always in the wrong and a crook who didn't deserve the air she breathed.

I kind of gave up on changing his mind regarding that. It didn't help me to make him mad. It was always better to keep him calm than to bring up a topic that he was so passionate about.

Weeks had passed since I found out about the acting governor and Blaze. A meeting with my mom was scheduled inside the prison. She said over the phone she would tell me more about the case and if it was progressing to favor her in the end or not.

I was excited to see her again. Meetings with her were almost nonexistent. That's what the law stipulated, and I hated it. I missed her and I was so excited to see her face again, even if she looked different from the independent woman I knew.

Celia parked her new car in front of my home and honked. I went over to her, got inside the car and she drove me to the prison. We talked about what I would talk to mom, and she said that I needed to be strong regarding everything that was happening in my life.

And I was being strong. If only she knew that I had become my bully's lover, she would look at me with different eyes. I kept that a secret from her, though. Didn't want her to think that I was mingling with people I shouldn't. She knew what happened every time I fell in love with a bad boy and he ended up dumping me in the end.

She parked the car at the prison and I was ushered by two guards to meet mom. It was the same room from the first time I met her. I sat down on a plastic chair and waited for her to come. She showed up a couple of minutes afterward, and I couldn't help but worry.

She looked so different from her usual self. It was like she was a different woman altogether, as if she wasn't even related to me anymore. She must have aged 10 years during this time she spent locked behind bars.

Were they even giving her food?

She sat down and picked up the landline phone that was the only way for us to communicate. When she spoke, her voice was weaker than it should be, "Darling, I'm so glad you've come to talk to me."

"I would come here more times if I could. They don-"

"They rarely allow criminals to meet people. I know. It's tough, but there is nothing we can do about that. We just need to make the most out of this meeting."

I thought about how I would word this, since I didn't want to give her another reason to worry about me. "Mom, do you suspect someone might have set you up?"

Her eyes widened. "What do you mean, Ariel? Do you suspect someone in particular? That is a possibility, but without evidence, we can't do much about it."

I couldn't straight up tell her I suspected Joseph Wadkins was involved. What if they were recording our conversations? He ruled over the state now and maybe he had some powerful contacts in the prison to do that.

"No, I don't have any suspects in mind. It was just something that crossed my mind. The one who benefitted the most from you being locked was..."

"The former Lieutenant Governor, who I like and is a close friend of mine. No, I don't think he's involved. He never came here to visit me, given that he has more things to worry about, but there's a reason why I invited him to be my Lieutenant Governor. I trust him."

If she did trust him, then I wasn't about to plant the seed of doubt regarding him in her mind. It was better to keep what I knew to myself. If she did suspect him, then maybe she could end up doing something stupid. She was so different now and wasn't the woman who I knew so well anymore.

I needed to protect her from whatever was happening.

"Okay, it's fine. I don't think he's involved with your case. Tell me, though. Does the lawyer think he will be able to find out what really happened, and that you are innocent?"

She leaned back on her chair, her eyes lost in thought. Then, she returned her attention back to me and said, "I think so, but it has been tough for him to make a lot of progress. He did find some odd things here and there he will have to confirm later. I think that my case might extend over this year..."

Oh shit. I didn't think it would take it that long to be resolved. I wouldn't be able to go to college without money. What worried me the most, though, was spending God-knew how long until we could be together again.

At this point, since I was kind of used to living in that house in the favela, all I wanted was to spend one day with mom, even if she was found guilty and couldn't get back most of her money.

"I hope he finds out what is going on behind all of this so that we can return to having a normal life together again."

She nodded her head, and seemed ready to change the subject of our conversation. "Tell me, Ariel. What has life been like over there? I know that it has to have been tough for you. You never had less than the best before this whole thing blew up on my face."

I tried to smile. "It has been alright. I made some friends and they are nice people."

That seemed to have calmed her wrinkles. She had so many of those now. I was beginning to hate this whole prison.

"What is he like?"

Her question came out of nowhere, and it faded my fake smile. "What do you mean?"

"Oh, Ariel. Don't you think I can't read you. I know when someone is in love."

"I–I–"

"Don't worry. I won't tell anyone about him. Just tell me what he is like and his name."

I swallowed hard. "I met this guy in school. His name is Blaze and he has been protecting me over there. He's... really nice and we have been together for a couple of months now."

She nodded her head and grinned. "I'm so happy you are growing up. I wished I was out of this prison so that I could better guide you. You've had so many bad boyfriends in your life."

"Thanks, mom, but I think that he will be different from them."

She chuckled. "If you say so. You are the one who has been spending time with him. I will trust your judgment. If he does anything you don't like, you tell me next time you come here, okay?"

I grinned. "Next time we meet, it won't be here."

And with that, we ended the serious part of the conversation and then talked about more mundane things, like my test scores, how well I was doing in school, and Celia and how much and how often she was helping me.

Being locked up like this made mom worry so much about me. She didn't think I would be able to handle life on my own. Celia was a big help and mom did prepare me for a life without her, even if she thought she didn't do enough for that.

Despite having so many workers to take care of me when we still had a normal life, I didn't forget to learn how to handle life by myself. Even if they thought they were pampering me too much, I was actually learning from them what to do in difficult situations.

Mom put the phone back where it was and she looked at me with sad eyes. I knew she wanted to hug me, but the prison wouldn't allow that. I also looked at her for a couple of seconds until we both turned and walked away.

Next time we were to meet again, it wouldn't be inside this prison. It wouldn't be in this horrible meeting room, and she would be able to kiss my cheeks and hug me.

If there was something wrong going on behind her corruption case, I was going to find out the truth.

I found Celia in the waiting room and, just like last time, she asked me if I was doing okay. I held my tears back. I was tougher now and more accustomed to my new life, but what was happening was still taking its toll on me. I hoped I didn't age too much since that party. Celia never mentioned anything regarding that, so I guessed I didn't have anything to worry about wrinkles and grey hair follicles showing up all of a sudden.

Celia and I talked about what happened during the meeting with my mom, but I refrained from mentioning anything regarding my discovery. If there was one person who I didn't want to involve in the case, it was her. She took care of me and it was dangerous enough for her to show up at my home from time to time to help me.

We got home and she made dinner for me. I messaged Blaze to tell him not to come and that I had to meet mom. His answer? *Okay. Be safe.*

He didn't mention how I shouldn't be thinking that mom was innocent again, and that was some progress. Important progress was being made in that department of our lives. I wished I could change his views regarding my mom, and maybe one day I would.

A couple of days passed and Blaze said, "Want to have dinner with me in a restaurant? It's one I've been wanting to go to for a very long time, and I was just waiting for the right trophy I could have to show off to certain people."

I wanted to slap his face, but only slightly brushed his shoulder with my fist while grinning at him. Blaze kept on mentioning that I was his and that he needed to show everyone that, but the truth was different now. He just didn't want to admit it right now.

"Of course I want to, as long as Gabriel doesn't come with us."

"Hey! I'm here and listening to everything you say," Gabriel said as his eyes warned me not to forget he was with Blaze much before I showed up.

Blaze turned his head to face his friend. "Just go, Gabe. I will talk to you later."

Despite the words that were spoken, our tone was a casual one. Gabriel knew we were lovers now and was okay with spending less time with his 'boss.' He might consider Blaze the most important person in the world other than his parents, which I never met so far, but he knew when to step aside and do something else when the situation called for it.

He settled his hand on Blaze's shoulder and said, "If anything happens like that time, don't hesitate to call me."

He was talking about that night when Blaze protected me from a stranger and ended up losing the fight that ensued.

"It's okay, Gabriel. Nobody will mess around with me."

His tone changed all of a sudden and his eyes got serious. "If *he* calls, call me right back."

Gabriel's tone also changed. "If that happens, I will let you know."

It seemed that whatever was their job, what they did when they weren't studying or spending time with me, had gotten serious these last few days. If they were working more, then my chances of finding out more about their relations to the lieutenant governor were now greater.

Maybe I could finally have my chance to find out more about mom's corruption case.

Gabriel shook his friend's hand and walked toward what I assumed to be his home. The sun was about to be replaced by the moon, and I didn't think he had anything to do other than to chill out in his house.

I was surprised that Blaze decided to take me to a restaurant. During our first few weeks together, when I was still nothing more than his trophy, he kept taking me to that warehouse in the docks where he and Gabriel chilled out at the sound of pop music.

Perhaps, without him realizing this, he was becoming more and more like me. I knew I was becoming more like him, considering my different lifestyle and the clothes

I now wore. It wouldn't be far-fetched to think he was going through the same changes, even if, for his case, they were more subtle.

"Ready to be my little princess and look beautiful for all those rich fucks?" He asked, his smile joking.

"Rich fucks? You aren't taking me to an expensive restaurant, are you? You know we both don't have the money for that sort of thing."

He ushered me to his car and said, "You will soon see, Ariel. I think that now I have more than enough money to spend on a more expensive restaurant. Maybe not the fanciest in this city and one of the restaurants you were used to before you moved over here, but definitely better than Wendy's."

And Blaze did take me to a fine restaurant. Its name? John and Noble Meeting Spot. It was a cozy place and the golden and orange-ish lights made it look romantic. Not a usual place for someone like Blaze, but he didn't look out of his element at all.

We found a table for us two and the waiter took our orders. We talked about mundane things, and he didn't ask about my meeting with my mom. That was a relief. It was better not to remember that he disliked her as much as he did.

The food was soon put on the table, and we ate it while talking about common topics between us. I was so glad I had him as my boyfriend now and that things took the turn they did. There was nothing like feeling protected by someone of Blaze's caliber.

Once we were done eating, I was feeling like we deserved this. After everything that happened in our lives, we deserved this moment of peace. I was so happy I didn't have to worry about what he would do to me anymore. Even if he thought he owned me, which wouldn't be too far from the truth, he wouldn't do anything bad to me.

Of that, I was certain of.

But once his phone rang and he looked at its screen, I knew something serious was about to happen. He looked at the screen for seconds longer than a person would for a normal call, and his smirk disappeared.

"I gotta talk to someone," he said before walking over to stand far from me, but not far enough to make it impossible for me to overhear some of what he was saying.

I shouldn't be eavesdropping on my boyfriend, but he did give me some reasons to do so.

I couldn't hear much, but I heard this, "... and yes, I will go meet you soon at Cliff Lane and Sun Way. I should be there in about ten minutes."

Ten minutes? That didn't leave me much time to get there and find out who he would be meeting up with. I needed to find out what he would be doing there and with who, though. It could be that he would be meeting the lieutenant governor, and if that was the case, I needed to be there.

If I knew the two of them were meeting, then I could press him to find out what they were doing together, and why the most important man in the state was meeting a favela boy like Blaze.

He came back over and sat down in front of me. "So, what was the call about?" I asked.

"Nothing. Don't worry about it."

His mouth said one thing, but his eyes told me something else. What he was about to do with whoever called him was important, and he would rather not involve me. Was he doing that so he could protect me? Or did he simply not want me to know something that was important to me?

We talked for some more minutes, but he then quickly got up and said, "I will drop you off in front of your home and then we will talk some more tomorrow, okay?"

I wasn't shocked. I saw this coming. Since the conversation he had over the phone, he felt like he was hurrying the rest of our meeting and wanted to go to that meeting place as soon as possible.

"Fine by me."

"You know, you have been acting like you are on the same level as me. Don't make that mistake," he warned with a smile on his face.

Despite the tension that grew between us thanks to that call, he was still the same joyful asshole I liked and knew so well. I couldn't help but hold his hand as he took me to his car. His idea was to make these people here - and some of them knew him and me - see that I was his.

But I felt that things were about to heat up between us. I wasn't supposed to sneak up on him to find out what his shady business was, after all...

# CHAPTER 8

## Digging In

Blaze dropped me off in front of my home, and having learned where he was going to meet whoever was on the other side of that call, I took a Uber ride to get there. I asked for the driver to turn off his headlights and to stop his car a couple of blocks before the place I intended to get to.

He was fine with those things and didn't ask any questions. I would rather not answer anything or talk about anything with him, and I was relieved he didn't get too curious about what I was set to do over there.

Upon getting closer to the meeting place, I found out I was already too late. Or maybe... not too late after all? The meeting was already happening. Blaze was leaning over the window of a black car. To my disappointment, the car's windows were tinted black. Under the darkness of the night, it was impossible to see who was the driver.

There were a lot of high-rises in the area, and I was thankful for that. It meant I could approach them without being seen. And that I did, and when I got close enough to hear what they were talking about, I hid behind a wall and only peeked sideways to find out if they were close to ending their meeting or not.

However, considering what I had just begun to overhear, it seemed that was far from being the case.

"So, you want me to do another job for you?"

"That's exactly why I hired you at that time and why I need you to help me take down another asshole."

"What's in it for me?"

"For starters, a lot of money, as usual."

So that's how he managed to pay the restaurant bill when we ate there. No wonder he had better clothes now. Whatever his job was exactly, the pay seemed to be pretty good.

I should hate him for the kind of job he had, but how could I? One of my greatest weaknesses was falling in love with the wrong men, and he ticked all the boxes.

"I see. Well, I'm willing to do whatever you want me to do. Some of the payment should be made in advancement."

The man inside the car, whose voice I couldn't recognize, chuckled for a couple of seconds. "You are learning your way around this business. It won't be long before I can make you a permanent employee of mine."

"As long as the pay is good, I will be around to help you."

I peeked sideways and found the man inside the car handing a note to Blaze. Blaze studied it for a couple of seconds and then stored it inside his pocket.

"Once the job is done, I will call you, as usual."

"Perfect," Blaze said.

And with that, the man rolled up the window of the car and drove off. To where? I had no idea, and I did notice his car didn't have a plaque number. Whoever he was, he was no novice in the kind of business he was dealing with.

If there was a moment to find out more about Blaze, it was now. I knew I was putting in jeopardy what we built so far, what he had become to each other, but my mom was more important than those things, and if there was a way to help her, I was willing to do almost anything.

What I came here to find out, I did. I needed to know what his job was, and it definitely was worse than I imagined. I didn't know all the details, but the pieces were falling into place. Blaze worked with an older man who had powerful enemies, and he used him to take them down.

I breathed out, trying to calm myself. I wasn't only putting our relationship in jeopardy, but also my well being. Despite being my boyfriend now, Blaze was still the same asshole who could almost do anything when he was angry.

This could be my last meeting with him where he wouldn't try to destroy me, and he could end up thinking I was his worst enemy now. Not a nice thought that was.

I got off the wall I was hiding behind and showed myself to him. He had already turned and was walking over to his car. His feet stopped, and his eyes shot wide. Blaze didn't expect to find me here, but his mind soon worked out what my presence meant.

His eyes returned to normal, but his face was paler than it should be. "What are you doing here?" His tone was rude, but it didn't make me more afraid of him than I already was.

"Finding out what your job is about."

"You shouldn't have done that. This place and my job aren't for princesses like you."

"If you didn't notice, I'm not your princess anymore. I care about you."

He laughed. "I'm sorry, but I don't need anyone worrying about me. I am my own man now."

"Yes, you do. What you are doing to get by is wrong and it will end badly for you."

A moment of silence ensued. "I don't want you worrying about me, and this will have consequences for you. Deep and painful consequences that you won't want to know beforehand."

"I'm not worried about them. I want to know what your job is exactly. You can't keep that only to yourself for the rest of your life, and you can't think the authorities won't eventually find out what it is that you do."

"I don't care about the police, and I'm not alone. Gabriel helps me out, as you should already know."

"Tell me this, though. Is your job something that involves me?"

That was the moment I waited for the most. Maybe I was being paranoid, but I needed to know, and I needed to study his reaction to that question.

And I waited. Seconds of silence ensued, and I thought I saw something in his eyes. Hesitation? Fear of what the information he had could mean to me? Whatever it was that flashed faintly across his eyes, it wasn't good, and it piqued my interest regarding his 'job' even more.

"It's nothing you need to worry about. Now, get lost, and don't expect me to be nice to you from now on."

He took a couple of steps toward his car, stopped and turned around. "And don't follow me around like this again. I won't forgive you a second time, if that happens."

And with that, he got behind the steering wheel and drove off. He left me alone when he could have dropped me off in front of my home again. Blaze didn't like what I did, but that only increased my appetite to find out more.

I had another plan, and it could mean the end of my relationship with Blaze forever, but it could be worth it, depending on what he was hiding.

* * *

It was the day after the encounter I had with Blaze, and he didn't come to talk to me. I tried to call him over the phone and send him messages, but it seemed he was far too pissed off to talk to me. That was okay. Whatever was happening in his life, it was more important than worrying I destroyed my relationship with him for good.

The clock announced 10 PM. I didn't know if Blaze would be in his house right now or not, but I needed to know where he was headed next. The man inside the black car told him to do something to help him take down someone I didn't know, and maybe now I could have the golden opportunity I needed.

And there was the fact I didn't know who the man inside the black sedan was. I didn't recognize his voice, but considering how worried I was during their meeting, it wouldn't be too far-fetched to think his voice sounded different than it truly was.

Now that I knew where Blaze lived, I could do one more thing to find out more about the case that surrounded his life. And I was going to do so now.

I got out of my home and took a Uber ride to his place. Celia didn't come home tonight, so I didn't have to worry about coming up with an excuse for getting out at this hour.

I asked the driver to drop me off a couple of blocks before Blaze's house. He didn't worry that a young woman like me was about to walk the streets in the middle of the night in this favela. Once again, I was thankful that Uber drivers didn't try to find out about things they had nothing to do with.

I got to Blaze's place and noticed some windows open. The lights were off, but maybe he was sleeping so that he could pull off his assignment later. I didn't know any detail regarding what the man in that car asked him to do. I was only making educated guesses.

Being careful was the only thing I could do right now.

I got to one of the windows and peeked inside his house. That was his living room and, across from it, was his bedroom. The door to the latter was slightly open, and I couldn't find out if he was there or not.

My heartbeat rate was higher than normal. I was nervous and could feel the palms of my hands sweaty. If I didn't control myself right now, this could not end well for me. I could end up finding out that Blaze wasn't only an asshole, but someone willing to beat up a woman, if he thought I was too dangerous to him.

I struggled when I gripped the frame of the window and propelled myself upward, but I managed to get inside his home nonetheless. Not the wisest of choices, but there wasn't much else I could have done. I then looked around and was assaulted by the familiarity of the place.

I was here only once and I didn't pay much attention to his house, but this was where Blaze lived, and I was still in love with him, even if he didn't like me much anymore right now.

I sneaked around his living room, trying to find the note that man handed to him. It had to be inside his house, right? I also worried not to make too much noise. I didn't weigh a lot, but I needed to control how I was stepping on the floor, which was made of hardwood.

I scanned his whole living room, but didn't find the note. That was unlucky. The next logical place to explore was his bedroom, which meant he could be there. Going there would increase the chances of him finding out I was here.

And I didn't want to find out what he was like when he was truly pissed off.

Either way, the thought of having a chance to help mom made me step toward his bedroom anyway. I noticed the slightly open door again and through the gap, I looked inside. His bedroom was on the other side of the door, so I couldn't know if he was sleeping in it or not.

I widened the gap by opening the door a bit more, and when my eyes landed on his bed and I didn't find him sleeping in it, I was so relieved I breathed out. I didn't even realize I was even controlling how much I was breathing this whole time.

So Blaze wasn't around, but despite relieving me, that could mean that his note also wouldn't be here. However, maybe with luck, it would be here and I would be able to find out where he was now. I was pretty sure the note asked him to do the job as soon as possible and he wasn't the kind of man to waste time when it came to things he considered important, like making more money.

I opened the door all the way and began to explore his bedroom. I opened drawers, pushed things around, lifted up his mattress, and pulled his desk to see if the note was behind it. But I didn't find it, and that made me think that Blaze could have taken the note with him.

Why would he do that, though? Or maybe he burned the note to get rid of it? Now that I thought about, that must have been what he did! He knew I was curious and maybe he was paranoid enough to think I would try to find out where he headed to.

If that was the case, then I wouldn't be able to do anything to find where he went. I should have pressed him more when I confronted him yesterday night.

I walked over to his kitchen, which was in the same room as the living room. And I did notice a piece of burned paper on the stove. I rushed over to it. That had to be the one, right? The piece of paper that the man in the black sedan gave to him...

Maybe Blaze was in a hurry when he burned it, which would explain why it wasn't burned completely. Perhaps, the job that was given to him was more important and urgent than I initially thought.

Whatever happened, I was in luck. The piece of paper wasn't completely burned. There was a small part of it that could be read. I grabbed it and tried to make sense of the words, but... I soon found out that they were nothing more than a jumbled mess.

Or maybe it wasn't meant to someone like me. Maybe there was a specific code that Blaze and that man inside the black sedan used to communicate. Considering how important the job was, it wouldn't be far-fetched to think that was the case here.

But... who could help me out with this? Gabriel was most likely with Blaze in their mission. And he wouldn't help me out anyway. Oh fuck, things weren't looking up to me. I thought I would be able to help mom out, but it seemed that this was as far as I would get with this.

And I would never be able to find out what the current governor's involvement was with Blaze...

I didn't have anything to lose right now, and I did have Gabriel's number... If he didn't pick up a call that I was thinking of making to him, then that would mean he was with Blaze. Blaze, in that case, would probably end our relationship for good.

If, however, Gabriel picked up the call, would he even help me decipher these words? Would they even be enough to help me find out what was going on here, where Blaze went to? I didn't know, but I was desperate.

And with those things in mind, I picked up my phone and dialed Gabriel's number. The phone called him, and called, and called some more, and I thought that he wouldn't pick up and that he was with Blaze right now, when... he did it, and I was so shocked I thought I was about to have a heart attack.

"Ariel, what do you want at this time of the night?"

"Wait, you are not with Blaze?"

"Why... would I be with him right now? He didn't call me to do anything with him."

Oh fuck, this was my chance.

"Can we meet up in person? I need your help with something. Blaze could be in danger."

Maybe he was, considering that he decided not to bring his bodyguard with him for that particular assignment. I worried about him, despite working behind his back to find out what he was doing. Sometimes, a man could be too stubborn for his own good and needed a woman willing to cross some lines to save him. I wished that was the case here so that he wouldn't be too pissed off at me when I showed up wherever he was right now.

"Suuuure thing, I guess. You don't know where I live, right? I will head over to your place."

"Thanks, Gabriel. I will be waiting for you."

I took another Uber ride home, and when the driver dropped me off, it didn't take Gabriel long to show up at my doorstep. I opened the door and found his worried eyes. They studied me possibly to find out what it was that I was involved with.

"Come inside," I said before closing the door behind me.

"What is going on, Ariel? You should be sleeping at this time of the night."

It was past 11 PM and yes, I should be sleeping right now because of the classes I would have tomorrow morning, but I didn't care about them. This thing I was dealing with was way more important than them.

I showed him the note that was mostly burned. "Do you know anything about this?"

"Wait, where did you find this?"

A moment of silence ensued. I needed to be sincere with him.

"Inside Blaze's house. I sneaked inside it to find out what he would do tonight."

"Why did you do that? I thought you two were lovers now."

"It's complicated, but I think he might be in danger. You know how stubborn he can be sometimes, right?"

"Boy, don't I know?" He said with a half a smile on his face.

"Then, help me decipher this message. We need to find out where he is headed."

"Okay, cool. I am worried about him. If he went off to finish another job for that guy and didn't involve me, then it's more serious than anything we did for him before."

When he grabbed the note from my hand, I gripped his wrist and asked, "About that, who is that man?"

"Why do you want to know about him? He is nobody you need to be concerned about."

"The more people try to make me think I shouldn't worry about something, the more I do."

Another moment of silence filled the atmosphere. "Okay, fine. His name is Willian. I don't know if that is his real name or not and honestly, I couldn't care less. All I know is that he asks us to do some things for him from time to time, and he pays us quite well."

"What kind of things?"

"I think I've already told you enough, Ariel."

He tried to jerk his forearm free, but I kept my grip tight around his wrist. "I'm not stopping now. I need to find out what is going on with Blaze."

"Fine, have it your way. We don't know the details of what he does, but he asks us to steal or leave documents inside some places. We usually invade the homes of the rich, and honestly, I don't care if we are hurting them or not."

I untightened my grip around his wrist. What he said... could it mean that Blaze and he did it? I couldn't believe it right now - not without more evidence.

Gabriel read the note and said. "Some of it was burned, but I know where he headed to, more or less. We will need to find his car and wait for him to come back to question him, and then we will know why he didn't involve me in that particular job."

Gabriel headed off and I chased after him. We took a Uber ride to the location mentioned on the note, and once we got out of the car, we headed to Blaze's sedan. He wasn't inside it, as we suspected.

Blaze leaned on the car and said, "As I said, now we need to wait for him to come back."

Minutes passed and I kept on checking the clock on my phone. How long would it take him to come back to his car? Unless he got himself into trouble and couldn't escape from it, he had to eventually make his way back to his red sedan.

We waited, and Gabriel didn't seem worried. He kept on looking around, checking the mansions that surrounded us. Most had their lights turned off and those that did have some lights turned on didn't seem that they had many people in them. This neighborhood was so peaceful compared to the favela I lived in.

And just when I checked the clock on my phone again, I heard hurried footsteps coming our way. I snapped my head toward the sound they were making and was shocked to find Blaze trotting toward us.

And he stopped once his eyes found us near his sedan. He walked over to us quickly and he seemed ready to punch the two of us multiple times in our faces. But he didn't do that and merely eyed us with distrust in his eyes.

"What in the world are you two doing here?"

"I can't speak for her, but I'm here to make sure you would come alive out of this job, and thankfully, you did," Gabriel said, his arms crossed over his chest.

"You are not supposed to be here, though. I didn't call you for this job because Willian specifically said I needed to come here alone. He didn't want anyone else to know about what I did here, and now... two more people know, so that's *fucking* great."

"Don't worry. We don't even know which mansion you went to. You burned most of the note."

"As if that matters now!" Blaze threw his arms up in frustration. "He might find out that you were here, and then stop calling us to do things for him."

"Calm down, Blaze. Nobody will find out about this and that we were here. Now, if you don't lower your voice and begin to talk like a normal human being, I'm pretty sure word will get around that some residents of this neighborhood were worried that some shady people were out in the streets in the middle of the night."

Blaze looked at Gabriel as he attempted to control his breath. "Fine. Let's go back to my home, and there we can discuss this."

Blaze got behind the steering wheel and drove us to his home. I was surprised he allowed me to sit inside his sedan, but maybe he only wanted me to be around for the moment so that he could clear some things out regarding my snooping around him.

He pulled over in front of his house and we stepped inside it. He closed the door with care and said, his voice calmer than when we were in that neighborhood for the rich, "What the hell happened and how did you find me there?"

I was the one who spoke this time, "I needed to find more about the man inside the car and I was worried about you. I love you, Blaze, and I can't live with myself if I think you might be in danger. What you do and your whole job... they make me feel worried that you might die one night."

His eyes softened for a moment, but they were worried again soon after. "Ariel, you don't need to worry about me. Worry about yourself. You shouldn't be snooping around my life. There's a reason why I own you, and that is so that I can control you and what you do."

"Alright, enough about that," Gabriel began to say, "What did you do this time that you didn't even have time to call me?"

"It wasn't that I didn't have time to call you, stupid fool. Didn't you hear what I said? Willian doesn't want someone else other than the two of us to know the details about that particular job he had for me. And before you say anything else, I'm not telling what exactly it was that I did there and who was the victim this time."

Gabriel ran his hand through his air. He was uncomfortable about what was going on. Meanwhile, I was thinking that this was my only chance to ask him what was in my mind. I needed to be direct with him, now that I knew what he did for a living.

I grabbed his hand and held it in mine. His eyes found mine and I could see how much he cared about me, even if he didn't want to show me that. "Blaze, I need to ask you something and I need you to promise you won't be mad at me."

He smirked. "What, princess? You think I can make promises to you now just because I took you to a restaurant with me and we had a sweet time there?"

"Stop joking. This is important. It concerns my mom."

He withdrew his hand so quickly it hurt my heart. "I don't want to talk about her. I don't have anything to do with that crook."

"Please, Blaze. You need to let me make this question."

His eyes locked with mine for seconds, but those seconds appeared to have been more like hours. Something was going on in his mind that impeded him from telling me what he knew, but what was that?

I needed to know, which was why I gave him a peck on his lips. Maybe that softened his mind and made him realize that he needed to tell me what he knew, even if he wasn't to blame about what happened.

His arms were crossed over his chest, but he then let them fall to the side. "Okay, ask away, but don't begin to think I'm to blame about what happened to her and you. She's a crook and she will always be one."

I approached him and locked my eyes with his once again, refusing to look anywhere else. "Did you sneak inside our home and plant evidence to make it seem she did the things she is now being accused of?"

His eyes didn't widen. We all knew what the question was going to be about. Blaze's shoulders drooped and Gabriel went on to sit on the couch.

"I didn't plant any evidence. I went there and found some documents Willian wanted me to hand to him. I did what he asked of me and I was well-paid for that. If that was what allowed the authorities to find out about your mom's corruption case, then she's the one to blame for all the shit she did to this city."

I wasn't surprised or shocked. I kind of expected that answer all along, but what he said did push me away from him a little bit. And I even took a step back.

Blaze invaded my home and kept that a secret from me all this time. He wanted to punish me because of what my mom did, but he could have said something about what happened, right? I couldn't have been left in the dark all this time the way I was.

"I'm not sorry about what I did, Ariel, if that's what you are asking yourself right now. I did what I had to do to make ends meet."

What he had to say to me now mattered, but I didn't want to hear him. Why was this so difficult for me now? I didn't know. All I knew was that he was honest with me and wasn't his usual self. He was serious. He wasn't joking around with stuff he shouldn't.

Gabriel approached and tried to stop me, but I was already gone. I was gone from his house, out on the sidewalk, and ready to do anything that wasn't being near Blaze. I knew the answer or suspected that was one, but still... I didn't prepare myself for what it would mean to me.

By the time I was already walking away from his house, I was crying and controlling my sobs. Gabriel didn't come after me, but Blaze did. He gripped my shoulder and made me turn to face him.

I knew my eyes were red and I didn't want to show another weakness of mine to him. Not something I could control, though. And I wasn't crying only because this man, Blaze, invaded the privacy of my home, helped to destroy my former life, put my mom in prison and approached me while keeping what he knew a secret, but also because my mother was indeed... to blame for what happened to this place and that she wouldn't walk out of the prison before the end of her sentence.

"Ariel, I usually don't say something like this, but fuck it. I can't see you this sad and angry and bitter. It's why I approached you in the first place and if this helps... I didn't know I was actually going to meet you after stealing documents from your mom. I didn't even realize it was your mansion back when I got myself inside it. I'm sorry... I made you feel this way."

He was being genuine about those things, but there was a brick wall in front of us. He was distant, despite not hating me now as he should. Maybe he didn't care that much that I invaded his house, found out what he was doing and discovered things about his private life that I shouldn't. He was never a good guy to me, and yet, as usual, I fell in love with him.

But it was different now. My love for him ended the same way it did with all the other guys I once considered my boyfriends. And to be honest with myself, it would be more truthful to say my love for him was only shattered, but didn't stop existing.

Blaze was the only one who took care of me and introduced me to this new world that existed in the same city I grew up in. I shook my head and said, "Blaze... I can't talk right now. I don't want to talk. Leave me alone."

His hand reached out to me, but I had already turned and was running back home. It was going to take me an hour to get there, even when walking this fast. I was hugging myself and keeping my head low. I didn't feel like seeing the environment that surrounded me. It hurt my heart too much.

Blaze then caught up to me and put himself in front of me. "No, Ariel, you don't get to tell me what I should do. I know that what I do is wrong and that I was the catalyst that ended your former life, but you are... fuck, I can't hide this anymore. You are your own woman now."

That should have calmed me down, but it didn't. He stopped thinking I was his treasure, his object. I should be relieved he finally admitted to himself I was on the same level he was.

And yet, all I could think about was that he betrayed me. He should have told me what he knew about mom and me, and his prior involvement with us a long time ago. That was why he didn't tell me any of those things, right? He was afraid of how much the truth would hurt me.

"Blaze, I can't do this anymore. Give me some time to think, okay? I don't want to be near you right now."

"Ariel, I..."

But he didn't finish what he was saying. Gabriel showed up and led him away from me, one hand on his back while Blaze tried to look at me and find out what was truly going on in my mind. I was thankful his best friend knew what to do right now. We might not be close, but he could see things that Blaze couldn't.

And so I made my way back home. It took more time to get there than I thought it would. Maybe that happened because I couldn't think straight and everything hurt so much. Blaze and I were once lovers, and the new truth separated us now. I didn't think our relationship would end up being that short.

Maybe there was something to salvage from that, and perhaps he would show up again with a wide smile on his face to tell me he could help my mom after all.

What was I to do now? Blaze didn't want to tell me more about the issue, even if he was feeling bad now about his involvement. I felt like it didn't matter what I could tell him about mom, he wouldn't help her.

And most important of all, he found the evidence and it was only used to bring to the spotlights all the bad things she did.

I got home, closed the door and plopped down on my bed. I needed to relax and have a good night's sleep. My head hurt so much. My heart hurt even more. Maybe tomorrow I would have a clear head about what happened and devise a plan. I just needed to come up with something I could do.

Even if she was a crook and deserved to be put behind bars, she was still family and I wasn't about to give up on her.

And when the next morning came and I heard someone knocking on the door, I knew something even more important was about to happen.

# CHAPTER 9

## I Can't

My stomach growled in hunger and my head still hurt. My eyes felt heavy. I didn't want to talk to anyone, but whoever was knocking on my door was in a hurry. The noise he or she was making was loud.

I headed over to the door and slammed it open. I was so pissed off about everything that happened. But then, my eyes laid on the person I didn't think would show up all of sudden in front of my house. Blaze.

And it wasn't just that, he brought a box of bonbons with him. That was so unlike the asshole I knew. His eyes were filled with sorrow and it was evident he wanted to have a normal conversation with me.

"Can I come in?" He asked.

I was taken aback by his question, even though I shouldn't and already was expecting it before he said it. "Okay, s-sure. Come in, Blaze." My voice, from the outside, might have sounded calm and collected, but I was anything but feeling at peace with myself and him. A million thoughts were going on in my mind right now.

He smirked and came in, and I shut the door behind me. "If you don't like this flavor, I can go get something better."

He showed me the box, which I looked at and found out that it had bonbons made with my favorite flavor. Strawberry. I didn't know he remembered that about me. I told him only once what that particular taste of mine was.

I got the box from his hands and didn't quite know what to tell him. It was the morning after everything came crashing down on my head and Blaze just... showed up to tell me he was feeling bad about the things he did. Even if he wasn't about to straight-up tell me that, his actions spoke for themselves.

"Look, Ariel. I think we need to have an honest conversation, and I hope you won't hate me for this."

I put his box down on the couch and said, "Absolutely not, Blaze. I will never hate you..."

"No, Ariel. You've got every right to hate me after everything I did."

"I know that you were doing those things, did them, because it was the only way you had to make money and survive. I should hate my mom for having turned this place into what it is now."

He took my hand in his. "Look, your mom doesn't matter right now. I don't feel bad that she ended up being locked up because of me, but either way... I'm sorry I kept that secret hidden from you all this time. I should have been honest from the get-go with you. I knew who you were when I first met you..."

His words hurt me, but he was bringing me closer to him. I didn't think he would change so much in such a short time. Right now, he was treating me as his equal, and I wasn't his princess anymore.

"Blaze, let's just put together what happened behind us and let what has to happen, happen."

"What do you mean?"

"I need to talk to your employer, Willian. He needs to tell me what exactly he found in those documents."

His eyes widened. "That might not work the way you are hoping. He doesn't owe me anything."

"Yes, but... maybe he would rather keep you working for him than find someone else."

He was hesitating, but he eventually sighed and said, "Okay, I will make the meeting happen. He won't like it one bit, though, but... Gabriel and I'll be there to protect you from anything that happens, okay?"

I was overjoyed and kissed him multiple times. "Hey!" He said as he tried to breathe and control me.

I calmed down, and he said, "That doesn't mean he will tell you anything, that he will clarify what happened. You need to be prepared for the worst. If there's anything that we need to keep in mind about this, it's that your mom, and I hope I'm wording this right, isn't the angel you are thinking she is."

I gripped his hand tightly. "I know, Blaze. She lied to me this whole time as well. I need to have an honest talk with her regarding all of this."

"I will take you there. It's the least I can do after everything that happened."

"You don't need to. I can take the-"

"No, you will do this one thing for me, okay? You will come with me. I might be an asshole and you might hate me with your life, but I will do this one right thing and you will allow me to do it."

I grinned. "Fine, you bad boy. I will obey you like the little princess I am."

He lightly punched my shoulder and grinned back. "You will always be my princess."

And as he changed so much he could as well be a different person now, I knew the meeting promised a lot and that it might not deliver everything I was hoping it would.

* * *

The stars shone in the black sky, and we were graced by a first-quarter moon. Blaze was beside me, sitting behind the steering wheel as his fingers drummed on it.

Gabriel, as usual, sat on one of the backseats, and his eyes were alert as they kept on scanning the area.

Blaze chose downtown for this meeting, and we were all surprised Willian agreed with him. The first thing that Blaze said was that his boss wouldn't agree to meet with us, even when giving him a good reason to do so.

And we did have a good reason. Gabriel and Blaze said to him that there was a problem with one of the jobs that were given to them in the past, and that they needed to meet one another in-person to resolve it.

To say that I was scared and nervous would be an understatement. This was my chance to find out more and maybe even everything about what happened with my mom's corruption case.

The minutes passed and, eventually, the same black sedan with tinted windows showed up. Blaze looked at me seriously, and I nodded. I wasn't about to back down right now - not after going behind his back to find out what he was doing and if he was related to mom's corruption case.

Blaze, Gabriel and I got out of the car. We headed over to the black sedan with tinted windows, and one of the windows was rolled down. The face inside the car had to be from Willian, and he looked less than pleased to see me with Blaze and Gabriel. They did tell him they would be alone.

"What is the meaning of this? Do you want our arrangement to end?"

Blaze spoke before I could open my mouth, "This is Ariel Rummel and she has a couple of questions for you."

"I don't know what is going on in your head, boy, but I'm not in the mood to meet someone I don't know and answer her questions, whatever they may be."

I had to say something and I couldn't let him speak as if I wasn't here with them. "You know my mom, don't you?"

"What if I do? I don't care about her."

"Do you know former Lieutenant Governor Joseph Wadkins?"

His eyes froze for a second, but then he returned to being his normal asshole self. "If you want to find out if I have anything to do with him, you will have to do better. I don't answer questions from someone like you without getting something back in return."

"How about I not telling the police about what you do? Hiring men like Blaze and Gabriel to do your dirty work, and to steal documents from other people."

"Watch your mouth, piece of shit."

Blaze gripped my arms and made me turn so that I was facing him. "What are you doing? You want him to kill us right here and now?"

He whispered, but the tone and intensity told me how pissed off he was right now. We didn't agree that I would, all of a sudden, begin to threaten Willian.

"I have to do this! I can't let this man just leave without telling me what he knows."

Willian spoke, grabbing back my attention, "And I'm not going to tell you shit. I don't owe you anything and I'm sure you don't have any dirt on me. I'm sorry, but I think I'm done here. Gabriel and Blaze, we are done and don't try to contact me again."

"Wait!" Blaze gripped his arm before he could drive off. "Can't we cut a deal?"

"Cut a deal? Why?"

Blaze looked at me with worried eyes, like he knew that, in normal circumstances, he wouldn't be putting himself in danger because of someone like me. But he was different now, and I knew he wouldn't be able to sleep again if he didn't help me however he could.

"Just tell me, Willian. Did you hire them to steal evidence from my mom's house?" I asked.

He shook his head in disbelief and jerked his arm free from Blaze's grip. "I'm done here and if I change my mind, I won't hesitate to kill all three of you."

And with that, he drove off and we were left with nothing. We didn't get any new information from him. Even if Joseph Wadkins was his boss, he didn't show me any signs that could prove my suspicion regarding his involvement with my mom's corruption case.

I was left in the dark, and now my boyfriend was pissed off. "You should have been more subtle, Ariel. I don't have a job anymore and, fuck. I don't know what to do with my life from now on."

Gabriel ran his fingers through his short hair. "I knew that this meeting was a bad idea from the start. Who knows what Willian will do from now on. He might decide to kill us before we even do anything that might make him think we are going to tell the police about him."

I was disappointed, angry, sad and nervous all at the same time. "I just need to do something," I began to say, "I can't let him just disappear with all that information he must have. He hired you two to steal documents from my former home and I don't think he did that without knowing what those documents were. He knew he did that because it meant the end of my mom's political career."

Blaze looked defeated. Meanwhile, Gabriel had more to tell me. "You need to stop trying to find out if there's anything you can do for your mom. The documents are legit."

"Maybe you are right, but I need to clear some things up. I can't leave that one thing in the dark. It needs to be clarified."

Blaze grabbed my hands and held them in his. "You need to stop, Ariel. I hate to tell you this, but... your mom is a crook. Maybe you never noticed that, and that is alright. We all think our parents are the best people in the world."

His words hurt me and made me withdraw my hands from his. "I can't do that to my mom. I can't think she is a bad person."

Blaze settled his hand on my shoulder. "Maybe she isn't bad, but she committed a crime and you need to accept that her punishment is fair. If you want... I can testify against Willian, involve him in the case, and if the current governor has anything to do with all of this, we might make him commit a mistake."

"You think... that might work, Blaze? I don't think the current governor is stupid enough to do anything that might involve him in her mom's case," Gabriel said, his tone that of someone who was worried.

Blaze locked his eyes with those of his friend. "I think we need to do one last thing for Ariel, and you are going to hate me for this."

"I don't like where this is going, but... I'm with you to the very end, as always"

Even though I didn't have a single clue regarding what he was thinking, his eyes told me that there was some hope, and that he was willing to do something he shouldn't - something dangerous - to help someone he didn't care about.

He was willing to risk that much to help me, and I couldn't believe that he changed so much ever since I met him for the first time.

# CHAPTER 10

## For You, Everything

We found ourselves outside of the current governor's mansion. Not a place for people like us to be in the middle of the night. The best thing about living in a neighborhood like this, so isolated from the city was that any noise could be heard miles away. Chances of a neighbor seeing us here now were almost nonexistent, though.

"Blaze, are you really sure you want to do this?" I asked after grabbing his hand and holding it.

"We discussed this and made plans. It's too late to give up now."

"I agree," Gabriel began to say, "We shouldn't give up now. We have to do this. We don't have anything to lose, do we?"

"Other than our freedoms, that is," Blaze corrected him.

"Yeah, other than those, but either way, it's not like we were fully free, to begin with."

Blaze chuckled and let go of my hand. "I told you to wait in your house, though."

"I couldn't. I want to be here when you two come back from there with the information we need."

"If it exists, because maybe he isn't to blame. Maybe someone else hired Willian for that job."

"Maybe so, but I need to find out the truth about the current governor's possible involvement. I can't let him just take mom's place and live the rest of his life as if nothing had happened. He is powerful, but he isn't untouchable."

Blaze smirked. "We already ended the career of one crook politician and I don't like that Joseph guy more than you do. If he has done anything wrong, even if he has no involvement with your mom's corruption case, we might still destroy him and do some more good for this city."

Gabriel stepped toward us and said, "It's not as if we would be doing a lot. River Valley is fucked anyway."

Blaze grinned and turned his head to look at me. "Wait here. We will be back soon."

I gripped his hand tightly. "Don't be careless."

"I'm never careless, princess," he said before giving me a peck and walking off toward the mansion with Gabriel on his tail.

I headed back to where they parked the car. Tall bushes hid it from prying eyes. It wasn't likely that anyone would come out of their mansions and find the car hidden behind the bushes, but we were careful anyway.

I got inside the vehicle and waited. Waiting turned out to be easier said than done. I couldn't just sit still here while Blaze and Gabriel were risking so much because of me.

I was still impressed that Blaze changed so much. He wouldn't have put himself in danger in other circumstances. He really cared about me, and the more time we spent together, the more that became evident.

The stars and the new moon moved in the sky. I checked the clock on my phone and found out that not even 20 minutes had passed since they got inside Joseph's mansion. They said it wouldn't take them long, but I was betting on the opposite of that. Joseph's home was anything but small and simple in its design.

And I got so nervous that I eventually walked back to the mansion. Upon getting there, the only thing that relieved me was the silence. If they had caught Blaze and Gabriel, there would be sirens sounding in the distance as the police cars drove toward here.

I rested my back on the wall, closed my eyes and waited for them to come. How long did I wait? I couldn't know. I forgot my phone in Blaze's car. I should have brought it with me, but my mind was a mess and I wanted to do nothing but pretend I didn't just put the love of my life in danger because of someone who wouldn't even be benefited from this.

But mom needed to know the whole truth, and I wouldn't rest until I knew everything as well.

As if by magic, I heard Blaze's voice and saw him coming toward me. They looked like a grenade just exploded on their faces, but they were in one piece. They weren't killed or caught. I rushed over to him and hugged him until he grunted in pain.

"Damn, princess. You can hug like a bear. I will be more careful around you from now on."

Gabriel chuckled and said, "We found some documents. Not sure they will help us, though. We didn't have much time to study them. Usually, we know what to look for when we invade a rich fuck's mansion."

I grabbed the documents and took a good look at them, but I couldn't make out if they proved anything that made it clear he was involved in mom's case.

"Yeah, I guess we will have to study them," I said before we headed home.

Even though the documents might not prove anything, might not even be related to my mom in any way, hope still filled my heart. The horrible case that involved my life was finally about to be concluded...

# CHAPTER 11

## Justice Prevails?

The court was finally going to decide mom's corruption involvement. I was sitting on one of the benches in the courtroom, and Blaze and Gabriel were with me. Blaze held my hand in his, and he could feel how tense I was.

It turned out that the documents did mention that Joseph was the one who ordered the documents to be stolen. They did exist and were legit. Mom was no saint from the very beginning. I felt betrayed. She didn't tell me the truth, but I didn't hate her. How could I? She was the only family I still had.

Mom was sitting at a desk made of hardwood with her lawyer. We handed the evidence to him, and he said he knew how he was going to use it. I trusted him to bring the truth out and expose it to the light of justice.

The current governor was sitting on one of the benches in front of us, and I couldn't tell what he was feeling right now. Whatever was going on in his head, though, was going to feel the impact of what the truth held in store for him.

Blaze looked at me and said, "Don't worry. We will make sure that fucker over there gets what is coming to him."

"I'm not worried about that. I'm just tense."

He gripped my hand more tightly, and the judge came into the room. He sat down on his fancy chair in front of us, on an elevated portion of the floor where there was a large desk with piles of documents on top of it.

"I hate these kinds of places," Gabriel said, shifting on the chair.

I returned my attention to the judge, who grabbed some sheets of paper and read them. He put them down and said, "I think there's an important thing we need to consider, and I would like to have more guards in here."

Joseph stood up and said, his tone louder than it should be, "What kind of change? Why are new guards going to come over here?"

The judge gave him a disapproving look and he sat back down on his bench. "It's better for you, governor, to remain where you are."

More guards came into the room and positioned themselves next to the walls. It almost looked like they didn't want anyone to escape. I knew the judge knew about what the documents said, but he didn't have to bring so many guards to keep the governor in the room. Maybe he was just being extra careful.

It hadn't been too long since we stole those documents. Maybe he knew they disappeared and kind of suspected what was happening. The judge appeared to be a wise old man, and he wasn't going to let anyone escape from their due justice before his eyes.

He started to talk about the case, covered what happened and why we were all here, but he didn't say anything about the current governor's involvement. That was something I was sure he was keeping for later.

Everyone in the room seemed tense. There were a lot of people sitting on the benches, and they were other politicians and representatives from different news outlets. This was the end of a corruption case that became known country-wide. Nobody before did something similar to what my mom did. The sentence that was about to be given to her would work as an important example for any similar case in the future.

"Now, before I mention what the sentence is, there is something that came up recently which I need to reveal."

His eyes scanned the room and then they lingered on the governor. He was about to make the political life of this state so much more complicated. There would have to be new elections and the whole country was about to learn that the case was much more complex.

"The current governor, Mr. Joseph Wadkins, is involved with Mrs. Rummel's corruption, and the documents I have in hand prove that."

Everyone started to talk loudly all of a sudden and the judge had to lift his hand and say, "Everyone, please remain silent. I need to explain everything."

The room fell silent once again. "We all thought that this case was a complicated one, but nobody ever questioned how the documents which allowed us to find out what happened came to light, and recently, that mystery was answered. Everything happened fast and I barely had time to study the new information. Rest assured, though, that I did study them fully and know what I'm talking about. Governor Joseph Wadkins stole the documents from Mrs. Rummel."

Everyone started to talk among themselves all of a sudden again, forcing the judge to raise his hand a second time. "I need everyone to remain silent, or I will ask the guests to leave."

But the current governor was about to do anything but remain sitting on the bench as if nothing of what was happening didn't matter to him. He stood up and said, "I can't watch and hear this in silence. I need a proper explanation. I don't have anything to do with this case, and I require permission to check those documents myself."

The judge put the documents back down on his desk and said, "You can't give orders here as if you were the chief of police. I suggest you calm down and remain silent."

"That's bull-" He was saying before his lawyer gripped his arm and made him sit back down on his chair. They murmured and had a heated discussion until the judge grabbed everyone's attention again.

"I know you are all worried, and the new case will be sorted out and explained soon. As for Mrs. Rummel, her sentence is what I initially set. Eight years in prison, and I now ask the guards to take her back to her cell."

Mom held her head down as the guards gripped her arms and started to take her out of the room. I wasn't sure what she was more disappointed about, if it was the revelation that her former lieutenant governor worked behind her back to bring her down or the fact that she refused to tell me that she did all of what she was accused of.

I was still going to meet her later, and we were going to have a proper conversation together. There was so much that she needed to tell me.

* * *

It happened sooner rather than later, and she looked more defeated than her usual new self. "Mom, you should have told me everything from the start, and I think... I should have told you something that you need to now know."

She raised her head. "What do you mean? You don't have anything that might save me from prison, do you?"

"No, you can't leave prison without serving your sentence. It can't be changed or made null. I... know where those documents showed up from and who got them. The ones which linked Joseph to your case, I mean."

"You were the one who found them? But how?" Her eyes shot wide in shock.

"I wasn't the one who found them. During my time in River Valley High, I fell in love with Blaze. He's fantastic and you will meet him one day. He's the one... who found the evidence inside our home. He didn't know this, but he worked for Joseph before I met him for the first time..."

Her eyes blinked a couple of times. "I have no words."

"Mom, I'm really sorry I didn't tell you those things before today. I didn't have much of a choice. Blaze wasn't exactly forthcoming with the things that he knew and didn't tell me them until I pressed him. I guess that it's a common thing now in my life to have information that should be exposed but remains in the dark because we are all so afraid of what it might cause."

"Actually... I am more surprised that you and he didn't break up yet. You've had so many boyfriends that hurt you."

I blushed. "Ohhhh... thanks, mom," I said before chuckling. "He's a really great guy and I can't wait to-"

"Marry him? I guess... I won't be there," she said before lowering her head.

"No, we will wait. It will take a lot of time and we might change our choices regarding what the marriage will be like, but we will wait for you."

She raised her head again, a half-smile on her face. "You should be hating me, but you are not."

I settled my hand on the glass panel that separated us. "I don't hate you. You are the only family I have."

We talked some more and I then returned home. That was that, then. Case closed, and Blaze and I didn't have to worry about anything else. Willian wouldn't come after us and he didn't know we were the ones who put his boss in jail. And I had a feeling they didn't like each other much anyway.

I saw Blaze waiting for me in the next room, and we kissed again. His own way to comfort me in this difficult time of my life...

# EPILOGUE

## No One Better For Me

Years passed, and everything was ready. Mom finally got out of jail, though her political career was pretty much over at this point. Who in their right mind would want to vote for someone who was put in jail for being corrupt?

I was somewhere I never thought I would be at. The church looked so beautiful. Of all the places Blaze could have chosen for this event, for this marriage, he chose this one. He was right there, waiting for me, alone as usual.

I didn't have a dad with me anymore, so the one who was taking me to him was Celia. I knew some people would find that odd, but it wasn't like I had much of a choice. A small detail that was, though. It wasn't like she was going to be with me for a long time and once she dropped me next to the altar, only Blaze would matter to me.

I couldn't hide my excitement, and I kept on fidgeting. "Calm down, Ariel. It's gonna be fine," Celia told me when she noticed I couldn't stop moving my fingers.

I grinned. "I've been waiting for this moment for such a long time. I can't be calm right now."

She grinned back, probably remembering what her own marriage was like and what she felt back then.

I looked at Blaze. His black suit was made for a proper marriage, a marriage like this one, it made him look even more stunning. His blue eyes caught my attention even from these many feet away. No wonder I fell in love with him.

I just didn't think he would ever be the kind of man to agree to a marriage. But he did change as time passed, and what was happening now was only a reflection, a consequence of that.

Even though music wasn't being played, everything was so loud and there was so much noise all around me. People who I knew and some who I was meeting for the first time greeted me as they entered the church to find their seats. I waved back at them with my hand and counted the seconds until the marriage would start.

I could see mom sitting on one of the front benches, and she was looking at me. Even from afar, I could see how much this moment meant to her. We spoke using our eyes only. She wished she was the one taking me to him.

Despite knowing who Blaze was, she liked him. I never thought she would ever approve of someone like him, much less accept that I was about to marry him. Her time in prison changed her. She was a different person now. Old things that held her life back were now in her past.

When she got out, it was like we found a light at the end of the tunnel that surrounded our life, that made it what it was. I had missed her so much. I cried night after night, thinking that her career and life would never be the same again.

What she told me changed everything. "It's fine, Ariel. I will find something else to do. I wasn't only a politician and I did learn some things along the way."

The only problem was that she needed to find a job where her identity couldn't be shown. And she did find something that was perfect for her. She was a writer now. I knew that was a crazy new thing for her to try, but she wrote so much during her life and despite creative writing being something different from her political pieces, she was doing well. Her fanbase was growing by the hour.

As for Blaze, he finished college. I couldn't believe he was accepted into the University of California at San Diego. He was so happy he cried, and I cried with him. His major was Engineering and he chose to specialize in Mechanical Engineering. He had some job offers already. He graduated no more than a month ago. Everything was happening so fast.

As for me, I graduated in Psychology. Not the best major for job finding, but it was a dream of mine. I always wanted to treat the minds of people, to help them find the right way, and even though my office was in my home because I didn't have money to rent one elsewhere, I was already excited at the prospect of becoming a proper psychologist.

Gabriel was also sitting on one of the front benches and he did wear a dark suit for this occasion too. He didn't change much as the years passed, and decided not to go to college. He still worked on some shady deals to make ends meet and he was quite successful in them. I was surprised he had the money for the suit and that he lived in one of the most expensive apartment buildings in downtown River Valley.

As for Joseph Wadkins, he was still in prison and someone else now ruled over the state. Someone better, who my mom liked. They had secret meetings from time to time. I didn't know what they talked about, but if there was one thing my mom could share with the new governor, it was how to run California and bring the best out of it. She did buy off the parliament so that her projects would be approved, but she still had a political experience that the new governor could benefit a lot from.

The marriage song finally began to play. I felt goosebumps all over my body. The marriage was about to happen, and I would stop being Ariel Rummel. I was about to become Ariel Janney. I could barely wait to become a new woman.

Celia began to take me to him and we crossed the entrance of the church. People stood up and started to clap. The sound that generated alongside the marriage song made me remember all the marriages I was a part of in the past, and how I wished that I would be the bride one day. Well, that was happening now.

I couldn't hide my happiness, and so I started to cry. Celia shook my arm a little bit, asking me to control myself. But that was easier said than done. Tears continued to roll down my cheeks as if her little complaints actually made me feel like crying even more.

The crowd got so loud. They must have noticed I was crying and how much this moment truly meant to me. There was nothing like marrying the man of my life, and I was certain I would remember every second to the utmost detail.

We continued to walk until we reached Blaze. His mom died and his father left him before he was a teenager, so it was no surprise that he was all by himself on the altar.

That was alright, he once said to me. He wasn't bothered that he became a man all by himself. Likewise, Gabriel was also alone on the bench he was sitting on, except for the strangers who sat beside him.

Celia stopped and allowed me to walk to Blaze, whose smile widened. She grabbed my hand and said, "Don't forget the words."

I whispered, "I won't."

Blaze grabbed my other hand in his the moment Celia walked to sit on one of the front benches. She worked so hard to make this marriage happen. Her eyes widened when I told her that Blaze and I were in love and that we wanted to marry each other. During most of my last high school year, she didn't have a chance to meet him. I should have introduced him to her once I knew that he was a good man.

"I think there are some people here who can't wait for us to say the words and finish this marriage so that they can all eat the cake," Blaze said, joking as he did so.

"Obviously and they will be surprised by the cake. It's one of the best I could have bought."

Since mom's sentence ended, she started to make us a lot of money. I wasn't as rich as before everything happened, but I liked my new life and, ever since getting used to living in a favela, I knew what humility was like and how important it was.

The father began to conduct the marriage. He cited the words he knew like the back of his hand. He was positioned beside us, and Blaze was in front of me now. His eyes looked at me, and they told me only one thing. I was his woman, the only one he needed in his life, and there was no else he would rather be with at this very moment.

I wanted so much to kiss him right now without even waiting for the priest to finish saying the words. There was something about this moment that also made me feel nervous, that maybe it was all a dream and that soon I would wake up.

But that was absolute nonsense. This was no dream. This was as real as the warmth that emanated from Blaze's body.

I picked up the last few words that the priest said. Something about rings. I knew what he meant and immediately allowed Blaze to put the marriage ring on my finger.

When he was done, I did the same to him, and I pressed his hand slightly because I loved him so much.

The priest looked at us with happy eyes, a grin on his face, and then said, "And now, you can kiss the bride."

Blaze embraced me as he kissed me, and it was like fireworks exploded in my mind. I wasn't just a woman now anymore, I was his woman for the rest of our lives, and our love felt so strong I was sure there was nothing in the world capable of separating us.

The kiss must have lasted for far longer than it should, because the priest was nudging me to stop it and continue the marriage. I gave him an awkward smile, and Blaze did the same. All that was left now was to walk back through the entrance and start our new life.

And that we did, and there was so much hope and happiness in my heart. I was so happy I cried once more...

*Don't go just yet...*

---

*You can sign-up to my mailing list to be invited for an ARC review and informed when a new book is released.*

---

# MORE LIKE THIS

## Stop Running: A Dark High School Bully Romance

http://mybook.to/running_stop

My feet were running on the sidewalk in a rhythmic, not-at-all methodic pattern. My body was slicing through the cold, unforgiving wind. My mind was thinking about how good it would be to be cozy next to a fireplace right now. The sidewalks and the roads were so silent one could think I was in a ghost town.

But that was far from being the case. Hope City was no place for beings from the otherworld. Normal people lived here and they were all sleeping now, waiting for the alarm of their clocks to tell them they needed to wake up.

My chest was heaving. I was running this whole time. It could have been for hours at this point, but I didn't care. I just wanted to find a safe haven right now, where nobody could find me and have difficult questions for me to answer.

I had a plan. A guy was going to help me. He said he would do so and, so far, he didn't fail to deliver on his promise. I needed the docs he would hand to me. I just needed to find the place where he said he lived.

And I was also terrified to meet him again. He was a despicable human being.

But I didn't have much of a choice. It was either that or going back to where I was, and I would never get back there.

I was panting so much I could feel my vision blurring. I found an alleyway and hid in there. I heard some hurried footsteps and cars running by, but didn't worry that they would find me here.

They were looking for me in places where they thought a young woman my age would be, and that was a big problem for them. I was anything but a normal 18-year-old girl. I had done things and experienced life events that changed me forever.

My mind was so different from what their shrinks thought I was.

I looked at the side and found a couple. A woman and man, and they were fighting. Heated words were being exchanged until the guy slapped her in the face and she fell over on her ass.

Hope City would never change. Those people were most likely high on drugs.

I heard the cars and people in a hurry disappearing in the distance and concluded I was safe, for the time being. I began to walk again and felt how refreshing that was. I had been running for a long time since my escape. I was so afraid those people would find me again.

I could never return there... That was the worst place for a woman like me to be. What I did, I did because it was right. They didn't have the right.

The guy who I had to meet here said he would be on a street nobody would like to be at this time of the night. He also mentioned it didn't have street lights and that it didn't have enough space for cars to park.

Hope City was established back when the country was born. Despite being small-sized and the fact that most of the people here were looking for a better place to live, it was pretty old. Most of the buildings were European-ish and most of the roads were made for people, not for cars. Even the sidewalks had cracks and weren't uniform. It was almost like walking in a European city, except that Hope City didn't have the good things that made those places unique and worth visiting.

I crossed one street and looked at the plaque with the road's name. Clove Street meeting with Plaza Passage. A rush of warmth flooded my heart. I was close to finding that guy's place and a way out. He said that they would never be able to find me because of what he concocted for me.

I hated the man, but if there was one thing he was good at, it was at being reliable with supplying fake documents.

*Okay, so from here, I just need to head left and I should find the street where he said he lives...*

His road didn't have a name - that's what he told me. He also said it wouldn't be too hard to find him because it was the only street in the whole neighborhood that looked like the entrance to Hell.

And so I headed left, my ears ready to pick up anything that should concern me. Even if I were safe from the people looking for me, there were still so many dangers in this neighborhood. This was where people sold and bought drugs every night.

The more I walked in here, the more I noticed that. I hated being in this place, but since I didn't have much of an option here, I would have to endure the time I needed to spend here.

But then, I would find somewhere better. I was sure of that. With those fake documents, I could do anything. And, I was already preparing a plan. There was something I was sure it would work well for someone with such a high profile as me.

And I found the dark street where even all the houses and buildings had their lights turned off. I wished I had a flashlight with me here, but that wouldn't be needed. The street wasn't long and there weren't many houses for me to check before finding the one where the guy lived.

Plus, he also said his house number was 69, so that was an impossible thing to forget.

I walked down the street, looking down most of the time to make sure I wasn't going to trip on something - even the road itself was all broken. It was like nobody from the city hall ever cared to fix this place.

The perfect spot for a man like him this was, though.

My eyes finally caught sight of the number and the house I was looking for. Even though it was dark, I could still see the place. It didn't resemble a house at all. It was more like a one-floor building or something like that.

It was very unique and somewhat terrifying. Someone who dared to enter the premises would have found that the reason they needed to turn around and run away as fast as possible.

I had a mission here, so I didn't have a choice.

I walked over to the front door of the house and knocked. I was calm after hiding in the alleyway, but now, my heart was uncomfortable once more. I had good reasons for that, though. This wasn't my first time meeting that guy and he was probably going to make me do... those things again.

I almost threw up, but held back the urge to do so. I didn't want to put myself in a weaker position before him, especially when he didn't even show up yet.

I looked around, uncomfortable and impatient he didn't answer the door yet. I knocked again and this time, as if he had just transported himself there, he opened the door. The gap was just enough for him to look at me.

His eyes widened and then returned to normal. He removed the metal thing that kept his door from opening all the way and opened a smile. His smile didn't change one bit, but what did change was my reaction.

I contained it, but deep inside my heart, I felt the urge to kill him right here and now. I also wanted, almost more than anything, to punch him hard in his face and continue to punch him until his body was motionless on the floor.

Renzo was of Italian origin. He was tall and fat, and he wore clothes that were too dirty - even for a man like him. His smile showed his yellow, decaying teeth and his face was so dirty to the point of being brown - it was almost like there was a layer of something disgusting covering it.

If there were three words to describe him, both in terms of his physical appearance and his personality, those would be 'piece of shit.'

"Hey there." his arm was resting on the doorway. "Came here for a special delivery?"

"More like a pickup." I entered his house without being invited, pushing him to the side because I didn't have time for a pointless conversation with him now.

"I have the *things* ready, but I want to know how you have been."

I spun around and met his eyes. "How I have been? I was running this whole time for my life."

"Oh, come on. It wasn't that bad. I made sure you would have what was needed to come here. You found me without a problem."

I scoffed. "As if that was what really happened. You didn't see everything. You aren't me and you never will be. You have no idea how many close calls I had during my escape."

"Well, my little darling. Some things can't be achieved without effort."

"Anyway, do you have the documents?"

"All ready for you," he said before putting his hand on my back and guiding me to his office, where he had enough computers and phones to make one think he was some kind of a mad man.

He was no mad man, but he was pretty close to that, though.

He picked them up and also showed me on one of his phones the digital versions of the documents. "Check them out and make sure you like the new you. I won't be able to change anything again, though. This is as far as I can help you."

I checked the information on the screen and the papers. "Okay, so my new name will be Katrina Whited? Are you sure this information will be enough for me to hide from them?"

"I helped to get you out of there, didn't I?"

I nodded. He was a despicable, ugly old man, but he was reliable. I could trust Renzo with this.

Out of nowhere, he took the documents and the phone off my hands. "You know that you have to pay for this, right? Payment will be the same as all the other times I helped you, unless you have enough money with you now."

I tsked and looked down, eyes burning with hatred. Of course he would mention payment. There was never anything free with him. Renzo was a member of the Libertas and just like everyone else from that gang, he didn't do anything out of mercy.

"Come on, start stripping."

* * *

I woke up sweating. The light coming from his table lamp was weak enough to make me think there was some kind of weird power outage going on - the reason for that, though, was because Renzo never bothered to buy a new table lamp.

I was laying in his bed, his body so close to mine I could feel the heat. His snoring filled the room and made me want to run away from this place as fast as possible.

The only thing that calmed me down here was knowing that payment was finally 'made' and he didn't have a single reason to keep me in here anymore.

I looked out the window and saw the stars. It was still dark. I wouldn't be able to sleep here, and also needed to do a couple of things.

I turned in his bed to face him and loathed the man before me. This couldn't be a normal human being. This was like a subject of the King of Hell, and he had to have come to Earth to torment people like me.

My ass still felt sore. Son of a bitch did everything he wanted and I did nothing to prevent him. How could I? It was either that or him beating me up. I was an agile woman and I was confident in my self-defense skills, but when it came to fighting him, I didn't stand a chance. He was tall, fat and strong. It would be like punching and kicking a tall building if I had dared to say 'no' to him.

But the worst was over and at least he used a condom.

Slowly, I crawled off his bed and walked around in his house, going to his office where my documents and the phone were. The smell of weed filled my nostrils and made me want to puke. Drugs were things I knew well and dealt with daily, but I still hated them. To be honest, being so 'intimate' with them only helped me to loathe them even more than normal.

I got inside his office and found the documents and the phone. *Okay, so this is all I need for a fresh start and to hide in plain sight, where they wouldn't be able to find me.*

I used the hacked phone to access Faith High's internal website and logged my information in there. Doing so was easy and it was like following a tutorial. Renzo explained all the steps needed to hack into their systems and do what was necessary so that *they* wouldn't be able to find me there.

I headed out of his office and toward the front door - Renzo didn't need to know I was leaving. He was used to that sort of thing.

My eyes, though, had other plans. I caught sight of something sharp that glistened under the soft light coming from the window. It was a knife, and I approached it. I grabbed it and checked it out for some seconds, making sure it was sharp and that it could be useful for me.

But then, a wild thought crossed my mind. Renzo was a loose end now, wasn't he? And, I wasn't going to need him again. He was still sleeping and snoring like a pig. They could find me through him, and I hated him so much for having abused me so many times.

I approached him, knife in hand and my eyes locked on him. I could do this. I could kill him and remove the last loose end. He was the only one. They could find and interrogate him. Their methods would be more than enough to break a man like Renzo.

And... I would be able to get my revenge. That was almost as important as removing the last loose end. Even though he knew what my past was like and why I had to interact with a man like him, he still used that to take advantage of me.

I was probably the only woman he ever fucked, considering how despicable he was and how he made me feel like throwing up.

And so, I made a decision. My knife in hand and ready to be used...

The next day, I was right in front of it. The school stood atop the hill - the highest point in the whole town. People who didn't know that this was a high school often thought that it was actually a castle, which would be crazy, as that would mean it was the only one in the whole country.

The place did look like a castle though, but it also looked like an enemy horde invaded it and then didn't bother to clean up their mess. The whole place looked like it needed a makeover. There was nothing about it that seemed new.

To be honest, Faith High School was probably even older than Hope City. That was something I would have to check on later to be sure about, not that I cared much.

I only needed to spend a year here in hiding before moving on to a better state where those guys wouldn't be able to find me, though. I needed to find my mom…

I walked through the front double gate made of rusted metal. Even though it wasn't moving, it still creaked because of the cold wind. The wind wasn't strong or anything like that, but it was moving with enough speed to make the old joints feel the weight of the construction.

Some students were looking at me as if they were seeing a ghost, but I didn't care about them. I didn't come here to make friends and I needed to keep my head low. I didn't want to draw any attention to me.

I was nothing more than a girl about to have her last year of high school and that was that.

I walked to the admission office and felt the coldness of the environment. How did people study here? This was almost as bad as the place I was locked in. It was like this was a prison made for high-profile criminals.

I crossed the halls until I found the admission office. That took more time than I thought it would. This place was like a maze and it was going to take me a lot of time to get used to it. It had been some time since the last time I stepped into the premises of a school, after all.

I opened the door and had to wait in a line until the attendant was ready to talk to me. She had glasses and her hair looked perfect for a nerdy old woman, who she was, I imagined. She didn't smile and her eyes only told me how much she hated her job. Just like with everyone else in this city, she wouldn't ask to be fired, though, because it was the only available position for her. She would most likely spend a couple of years jobless if she were to try to find something better.

Considering the kind of students that studied here and her bosses, no wonder she didn't enjoy sitting behind her desk. It was probably like some kind of torture to her.

"What do you want?" Her tone was rude and unwelcoming.

"I am a new student here. Katrina Whited."

"Really? I thought admissions were over already. We are not accepting new students."

"Check your data, tables or whatever it is that you have there on your computer. Look up my name and you will find it there."

Her eyes narrowed, but she still looked at her screen and typed my name. Her eyes widened a bit and I assumed that she, indeed, found my name in there.

"Okay. That's very weird, but if your name is in our systems, then that means you are indeed a student of ours."

"Yes, I am."

"Follow me. We need to take your photo for the student card and deal with some paperwork before you can begin to study here properly."

I followed her to a room behind the one she was and took the photo. The student card was ready soon after and she handed it to me. I made a face because I didn't like how I looked in the photo. There was something wrong with how the lighting was set up or something like that - the shadows contrasted too much on my face.

I looked like some kind of a freak, but that was far from being one of my most important problems at the moment.

She led me to another room that had another person, and that worker handed me some papers for me to sign. I came up with a simple, but effective signature that I could remember for future occasions. I also made a mental note to train my new signature. It couldn't also resemble my old one. I really didn't want to leave a single trace for those people to find me here. That just couldn't happen. I wouldn't allow it.

Once the paperwork was done, and with my shiny student card in my pocket, we walked to the main room of the school. It had a big chandelier at the top and many stairs that led to different floors.

If outside this place looked like a rundown castle, inside it looked like Hogwarts.

"I will give you a tour, show you where the classrooms are and other things you will find useful. I know how this place can be confusing for first-timers."

I gave her an uncomfortable smile. It was like she read my mind about this place. The maze-like layout wouldn't be so bad if the place wasn't so cold. It was Fall, but inside here, it was as if the cold could find its way inside my skin and torment my bones.

"Off we go then," she said and her tone was as boring as before. The attendant wasn't going to be all cheerful now when she probably had better things to do.

She showed me the classrooms, which were spread all over the place, the laboratories and the rooms where the professors stayed in between the lectures. She also showed me the outside, where they had a soccer field and a place for students to run laps on.

It was a pretty standard school in terms of resources and what it had for the students and the classes, but the castle-like architecture made it so different from other schools it could as well deserve its own category.

She took me back to the main room of the school, where the giant chandelier was and then said, "I hope you learned more or less what the layout is like, *and* don't come here asking me for directions. I won't help you."

And just like that, she walked off as if she truly wasn't obligated to help me here. She probably was, but there was nothing I could do to force her to do something. I was lucky already she didn't try to dig deeper to find more about my real identity.

I grabbed a paper which had the location and the number of my bedroom. I would be living inside a dormitory, which was less than ideal, but I had to consider myself still lucky. *I wasn't going to have a roommate.*

I went over to the dormitory. It was called Alexander Hall and that also reflected the castle-like persona of this school. Everything here was old and looked as if it came from a distant past that not even the history books once recorded.

Upon getting there, I already loathed the place. The dormitory was only for women, and those were of the worst type possible. Rich girls who thought they were the best things to ever walk on this planet were outside the main front door, and I would have to pass through them to find my bedroom.

I did have my things with me too. I had a wheeled bag and it had some of my things, plus some others I got from Renzo's place, but it was mostly empty. Its weight was more than enough to remind me of that. Someone curious enough would put me in a tight spot if they were to ask me why it was so light. Those girls were used to bringing their whole bedrooms from their homes to this place.

There were also normal girls and the shy ones that distanced themselves from everyone, their noses glued to the screen of their phones or stuck between the pages of their books. Those, however, were also not the kind of people I wanted to spend time with here.

If I got lucky, I wouldn't have to deal with any of them, though.

I headed to the front double door and crossed the ocean of rich girls that stood next to it. They all stopped talking and I could feel their stares on me as they probably asked themselves who I was. People like them were used to knowing every single person in their territory, and this was their headquarters.

I ignored them and headed inside. Upon finding myself free from them for now, I headed to the second floor, where my bedroom was. Room 217. I found it and used the key to open the door.

I entered the room, put my wheeled bag at the corner and studied the place. *It won't be too bad to live here.* It did have everything I needed, except for a shower room. That sucked. I didn't want to take showers in the communal bathroom.

This was still better than living where I was, though. That place was even worse.

I lied down in my bed like a falling boulder. Ever since the escape, I didn't have time to rest, and I wouldn't have classes until tomorrow anyway. I got here in the nick of time. One day later and that attendant would have dug deeper to find out more about me. I was glad I didn't need any legal guardian to sign the stuff for me too.

And I fell asleep soon after, wishing for my life to get better from them on. The room was so cold and unwelcoming, though. It was like I was stuck inside a prison cell.

✳ ✳ ✳

I had classes in the morning and then went to the dining hall. Just like the rest of the school, it also reminded me of Hogwarts. That was one of the movies I had the luck of watching, but I also didn't have the opportunity to watch the sequels. I heard there were seven of them, and I wished I could watch them, but right now,  there were more important things to deal with.

There was still time until the next round of lectures started. With that in mind, I headed over to the soccer field and sat down on a short wall that kind of enveloped it. There were some students playing soccer and one of them caught my attention.

His body, his face and everything about him... Wait a minute, didn't I know that guy? Never shook his hand or anything like that, but I did see him on TV many times. He was *that* guy. His name was Allan Brown and he was one of the main players of the Jesters, the state soccer team.

He was their number ten. He was no more than 18 and he was already famous country-wide. I knew his backstory somewhat, but I didn't think I was going to study at the same school as him. That... was the best thing that happened to me so far.

I was a huge fan of him and never thought I would be this close to him. Once the match ended, a bunch of students ran up to him, their hands holding photographs and notebooks for him to sign. He also took selfies with them, and his smile was... *captivating.*

He was a star here. If there was one thing to make me feel safer about studying in this place, it was that. His light outshone and would continue to outshine any other light in here. I had one less reason to think they would find me.

I was holding my phone in my hand and kind of wished I could be just like the rest, like the normal students. I wished I could take a selfie with him too and show it to my old man. I wished I still had a proper family...

But just when I was going to head somewhere else, Allan Brown started to jog toward me. That couldn't be because of anything important, right? He couldn't be coming my way to talk to me... *right?*

*Continue your read here: http://mybook.to/running_stop*